MARGARET

Margaret Mahy was born in New Zealand and has loved telling stories all her life. She has published well over a hundred titles and won several major prizes and awards, including The Order of New Zealand, for her internationally acclaimed contribution to children's literature. She has twice won the prestigious Carnegie Medal (*The Haunting*, 1982, and *The Changeover*, 1984). Margaret lives in the South Island of New Zealand, in a house which she partially built herself, overlooking Governors Bay.

Also by Margaret Mahy
Twenty-four Hours
The Tricksters

And for younger readers
The Riddle of the Frozen Phantom

MEMORY

MARGARET MAHY

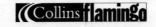

An imprint of HarperCollins*Publishers*

First published by J.M. Dent & Sons 1987

This edition published by CollinsFlamingo in 2002
CollinsFlamingo is an imprint of HarperCollins*Publishers* Ltd,
77-85 Fulham Palace Road, Hammersmith,
London, W6 8JB

The HarperCollins website address is
www.**fire**and**water**.com

1 3 5 7 9 8 6 4 2

ISBN 0 00 712337 X

Printed and bound in Great Britain by
Omnia Books Limited, Glasgow

CHAPTER ONE

Groping his way through darkness, certain he was no longer on the true path, Jonny suddenly saw a square of light appear ahead of him – the window of a house. His long scramble through unrelieved blackness was almost over.

Looking in from the road, uneasy in this odd rural area still so close to the city it did not seem like proper country, he had thought everything would be straightforward. The drive, well used and wide, had curved sleekly in under the trees. The solitary street lamp had illuminated the notice at the gate. *Rivendell Community*, it had read. *Kia Ora, Welcome.*

Underneath this were the names of the five families making up the community and there, quite clearly, it said *Carl and Ruth Benedicta and Family*. There had been nothing to suggest that, only a little way from the road, great trees would press in around the drive and that the cloudy night would become completely impenetrable.

"I'm not *that* drunk," Jonny had argued aloud, but nothing had argued back at him out of the darkness.

Now, however, there was a light ahead and, where there was a light, there would be a door to knock on. Someone would answer. Standing back in the shadows a little he would ask very politely if he could speak to Bonny for a moment. He went through the motion of consulting a watch which he knew he would be unable to see. Time was there, somewhere on the end of his arm, but lost in the dark.

Much earlier in this wild, shapeless night, in another time and another place, Jonny had sat down to a delicious meal with his parents and his little sisters, had even helped with the dishes in a cooperative, home-loving fashion.

"Five years ago today..." his father had said. It was hard for Jonny not to feel something reproachful in the simple words, as if he, Jonny, had no right still to be around – making jokes and plans – with Janine gone. The twins had continued to push and squeak, but all they knew of Janine was her photograph smiling from the top of the television set.

Jonny had hugged his mother, nodded a little doubtfully at his father and had set out to join friends who played in a band at a city pub.

Now he was stumbling in the dark, whirling with the mixture of red wine and brandy with which he had commanded a feverish lightheartedness, hoping to hold off attacks of memory. In between being wildly cheerful *then*, and lost in the dark *now*, lay violence and fury – a fight with sudden enemies, an argument with the police, and then another argument with his father outside the police station. A full evening!

Jonny thought he could hide his whirling state well enough to prevent any member of the Rivendell Community from being dubious about him, and it was important he speak to Bonny, for he was full of the ferocious questions which only revealed themselves when everyday reason was in retreat. Sometimes, just before waking or falling asleep, these questions haunted him for a second or two, allowing themselves to be glimpsed but never grappled with. He wanted to name these phantoms, and be free of them, and Bonny Benedicta might help him, for of all the people he knew, she was the most serene and the most magical. Besides, she had been a witness; she had pulled him to safety, had embraced him there on the top of the cliff, and had later told a calm lie that had certainly made things easier for him at the time. But then she had been shipped out of his life. The last time he had seen her had been across the chapel at his sister's funeral service. Their parents had talked while Jonny and Bonny simply stared at each other in silence. They were the only witnesses. Their statements for the *post mortem* had been taken down by the police and there had been no need for them to appear together in court. Never again, from that time on, even though they lived in the same city, had he seen Bonny Benedicta.

Jonny stepped boldly towards the lighted window, knowing there would be hundreds of traps and pitfalls for anyone wandering in darkness. Indeed, a moment later the dark exploded around him. Pale shapes, chuckling and crying out in unearthly voices, fled before him. Over in the direction of the window, large dogs began to bark, and within another moment everything had changed, for the moon, just past a quarter, surged briskly out from behind clouds like someone efficient arriving to put things right, and a whole yard directly in front of him was suddenly illuminated by a big outdoor light.

Jonny saw cars, a farm truck and a small cultivator, all drawn up before a huge shed. To his left the pale shapes, a flock of geese, hurried across the yard, necks at full stretch – alarmed and indignant. He could even trace the double row of walnut trees marking the end of the lost driveway. Overhead, the cloud which had successfully blocked out the moon for so long, was transformed into a huge silver lens brooding over everything below.

Jonny lightly touched his battered face as he walked across the yard trying to work out how much visible damage might have been done. One eye was swollen, though not entirely closed. His lips felt puffy. Everything hurt – and yet it seemed he was accidentally feeling someone else's pain. His indifference always made him feel hollow – not quite *real*. It was disconcerting too that, for Jonny, imaginary things, once properly imagined, could grow as powerful and lucid as if they were true. He had always been the victim of stories, not only other people's but his own as well.

I won't go in, he thought. I'll stand back a bit and ask very politely. It's a while since I saw the Benedictas, but it's not as if I were a real stranger.

Maori Land Rights said a big placard leaning against the back of a battered Volkswagen. Jonny sidled past it. Earlier, the city had been excited and restless. Cars had driven by, broadcasting messages, groups of people had been converging on the city square as he went into the pub with his friends, and, later, the police station had been filled with the arguments of young political activists. Jonny, who had been charged with disorderly conduct and summoned to the District Court once before in his life, felt like a veteran. He was not particularly interested in the small, fierce surges of street politics, yet here they were again, ten miles out of town, nudging him knowingly. *The Treaty is a fraud* said a long banner drooping between two sticks that were planted firmly by the small fence that separated the house from the yard.

Two German shepherd dogs were chained to their kennels on the lawn. The house, an old farmhouse, recently extended on either side, sprawled backwards into the shadows, but its verandah was well lighted and its door hospitably open. Ideally, Jonny would have preferred a little less light. He did not want anyone, particularly Bonny's mother, to get a good look at his face, not straightaway, at least. However, since he was wearing his bandit hat – an old black hat with a wide, slightly floppy brim – the worst damage might be hidden until a gentle voice and polite approach had made a good impression. Jonny vaguely knew that some people found him rather sinister even without the addition of bruises, and indeed he had sometimes found it an advantage when it came to fascinating certain girls. But tonight he wanted to seem as ordinary – as unthreatening – as possible.

"My face? Oh, yes. I took a spill off a motorbike..." he muttered casually. Jonny had always talked to himself, rehearsing what he hoped to say.

Bonny's parents were both doctors, but whereas her father was a doctor of philosophy, her mother was a pathologist, and she might be able to tell a motorbike bruise from the sort left by a fist with a ring on it.

"Nothing venture, nothing win!" said Jonny to the dogs. He had given up tap-dancing, yet his feet repeated the rhythm soundlessly, just from habit. Automatically, he smiled in the dark, just as if his mother were there prompting him. The dogs, missing the smile but detecting the syncopation in his step, were sure he was challenging them and, infuriated all over again, strained on their ropes longing to bite him.

Jonny, climbing the steps and rehearsing as he climbed, said, "Bonny, I've got just one thing to ask you." The door was before him. He imagined Bonny standing framed in the doorway, tall and mysterious, hair and skin like honey. "You'll think I'm a bit mad, but it's five years today... and we were the only ones who saw her fall... you're the only one I can ask..."

"Another one! You're late! I thought it must be someone when I heard the dogs so I turned on the outside light. Come on in."

It was not Bonny, of course. It was a girl he didn't know – short, with a head of thick, brown curls. Jonny tilted his bandit hat forwards slightly and spoke from under its dashing brim.

"I wondered if I could speak to Bonny, please. I won't keep her long."

"Who?" asked the girl. "I don't know many people here... Actually, it's the first time I've been here myself."

"Bonny Benedicta," Jonny said, lowing his voice a little. ("Speak in the lower register, Jonny," his speech and drama teacher had advised him a long time ago.)

"I don't know her," said the girl, "but the Benedictas do live here. Come in and find her for yourself."

"Great," said Jonny, "but I don't want to stay. I just wanted to see Bonny for a moment."

He had not planned to go into the house, yet, as she retreated, looking back confidently over her shoulder, he followed her through a hall that seemed to be lined with raincoats, gumboots, plastic buckets and even a few gardening tools. The kitchen into which they walked was brightly lit, big enough to dance in, partly intersected by a counter crowded with cups and saucers, papers, a telephone, a bowl of eggs with mud on them, and set around with red bar stools. The other half of the room was dominated by a large wood stove, rather like a kitchen altar, with two other girls hovering like acolytes before it. A little to the left there was a more conventional electric stove, unattended.

"Jill's the flowery one, Amy's punk," said the girl who had led him in, gesturing vaguely right and left. "I'm Polly."

"Jonny. Jonny Dart," Jonny said, as they looked at him with open curiosity, noting the headphones of his Walkman around his neck, his bandit hat, his gaudy, old, striped blazer.

"Isn't this a wonderful kitchen?" Polly went on. "A typical farmhouse kitchen."

"Correction," said Amy. "A farmhouse would use the electric stove. The water would be boiling by now."

"Be fair!" said the other girl, Jill. "They've lived here for five years. It's not just play."

"Do you want a drink?" Polly asked, nodding at a collection of bottles on the end of the counter. Jonny looked at the bottles cautiously.

"I've had one or two already," he admitted.

"Who hasn't?" Polly answered, and began to construct a generous drink from gin and lemonade, dropping not just slices but whole chunks of lemon into it. Jonny took it obediently, though it turned out to be so strong his horrified throat tried to clench itself like a fist. ("You'll suffer for this," said a part of Jonny's mind secretly to the rest of him. "Oh, well, a short life and a merry one," the rest of him replied, showing his mind just who was in charge.)

"I wanted to speak to Bonny," he said for the third time, and Jill looked rather startled. At least she knew who he was talking about.

"Is she here?" she asked doubtfully. "I haven't seen her. She's not like Hinerangi you know…"

Jonny did not know who Hinerangi was.

"Well, maybe Dr Benedicta?" he asked tentatively. "Or Samantha…" he added quickly, as he suddenly remembered Bonny's younger sister.

"The doctors are through there," said Polly loudly, pointing to a door. "They're waiting to see the midnight news. There'll be reports on marches from all over the country."

"Is it midnight?" Jonny exclaimed, and was so horrified to hear the time that he took a large unguarded mouthful of gin and lemon. All the same, if he had been thinking clearly he would have known that it was very late to call on anyone. Yet it was almost as if he had been expected.

Polly peered up slyly underneath his hat. Her expression sharpened. "God!" she cried dramatically. Before he could stop her she had swept his hat away, and the three girls stood staring intently at him. The kitchen light in its plain, white shade shone down.

"What happened to you?" cried Polly. "Did the cops get you?"

"Court appearance Friday," Jonny repeated, rather mystified, however, by her quick understanding, and by the feeling of having thrilled them without meaning to.

"The pigs!" Jill cried. "They shouldn't be allowed to get away with it."

"Any law enforcement system is simply a tool of political control," remarked Amy. "Have you got a lawyer?"

Jonny saw that there had been a misunderstanding.

"They didn't *do* it," he said, smiling, even though it hurt to smile. "It was just a fight in a pub, a bit of hotbloodedness. You know!" However, he saw at once that they did not know.

"But the police *did* get you?" persisted Amy, apparently reluctant to give up this possibility.

"Well, yes – they broke it up," Jonny agreed, "and I wouldn't give my name. I thought I might get away with it." He might almost have been talking a foreign language. They seemed to be waiting for more. "That's it!" he added lamely. "It's not the first time."

They continued to stare at him, revising their first friendly opinion of him.

"Weren't you on the march?" asked Jill at last.

"No," said Jonny. "I'm a tap-dancer, not a marcher." He

drank a little more, although by now he felt as if he were watching them down a seething tunnel which was beginning to fall in on itself. Something was devouring the lighted edges of the room. When Polly spoke again she sounded slightly hostile.

"Well, what are you doing here, then?" she demanded. "We've all been on the Maori Land Rights march. This is a Land March party."

"I keep telling you," Jonny said patiently. "I wanted to talk to Bonny Benedicta." His feet seemed miles away from the rest of him, a shifty disobedient frontier where he had once been complete master. The girls glanced at each other.

"I'll ask," said Polly. She vanished through the door and, as she opened it, excited conversation on the other side rolled towards them, one busy sound made up of a lot of little ones. Jonny, irritated at having to hold a glass, drank the rest of his drink very quickly.

"I've often thought I'd like to do tap-dancing," said Jill, "but I'm not the dancing type – not really."

"Anyone can have a go," Jonny replied rather wearily.

The door opened, but it was not Bonny. It was her mother, Dr Ruth Benedicta. Jonny hadn't seen Dr Ruth since Janine's funeral. If he hadn't been struggling to keep the encroaching darkness from swallowing the room, he would have laughed a little at her involuntary grimace when she saw him.

"Do you remember me, Dr Benedicta?" he asked very politely, jiggling as he spoke. Automatically he smiled and looked happy, just as if his mother were standing in the wings, taking notes on his performance for discussion afterwards.

"Jonny Dart," he reminded Dr Benedicta, staggering.

"Jonathan Dart," she said almost simultaneously. "What on earth are you doing here at this time of night?"

"Sorry," Jonny said. "I didn't know what the time was. I just wanted to see Bonny for ten minutes."

Behind Dr Benedicta, Amy and Jill huddled by the wood stove. The water in the kettle sounded as if it were boiling, but neither of them seemed inclined to begin making the coffee.

"Bonny's not here," said Dr Benedicta. "She's flatting in town these days."

"Oh," said Jonny rather blankly. "I've lost touch..."

Dr Benedicta's eye fell on the glass at the end of the counter.

"Who gave him a drink?" she asked sideways in a low, cross, but entirely audible voice.

"Polly!" said both girls, quickly and virtuously. Polly had not come back into the kitchen.

"Well, could you give me Bonny's address, please?" Jonny said, monitoring his own voice as well as he could. "Or her phone number?"

"What do you want to see her about?" asked Dr

Benedicta, still sounding cross. "She wasn't a great friend of yours, was she?"

"She used to be my Pythoness," Jonny said, smiling. But when he saw how grim Dr Benedicta looked, he added hastily, "It was a game we used to play. She was the Pythoness. She prophesied and gave good advice, all in rhyme, too. Anyhow, I've got a present for her." He touched the pocket of his blazer.

"I assure you Bonny doesn't tell fortunes these days," Dr Benedicta said, ignoring his reference to a present.

"I know. She can't – not any more," Jonny agreed. "I just wanted to see her. It's a sort of anniversary. It's five years since Janine died."

Dr Benedicta began to look rather more sympathetic, but more as if she thought she ought to than because she wanted to.

"I suppose it is," she said slowly. "It's nearly five years since we came out here. Well, I don't know, Jonathan. As I said, Bonny's not here, and I'm sure things will seem very different to you in the morning…"

"It'll be too late," Jonny interrupted impulsively. "In the morning everything will change back." But she talked on, ignoring him.

"I don't want Bonny upset in any way. She's got a lot of work on her hands for her finals. And as you know, Jonathan, it took her a long, long time to get over Janine's death… She was really devastated."

"None of us laughed," Jonny remarked, opening his eyes wide, giving Dr Benedicta an alarming stare. ("Careful," he was telling himself as he spoke, hearing the aggression in his own voice.) The room seemed to be almost dark, though the light was on. Dr Benedicta's face seemed suspended in front of him, phosphorescent and stern. The two girls shimmered in the remote distance.

"Of course not," she agreed hurriedly, "but I don't think I'll give you Bonny's address until you've gone home and had a good sleep and are in better condition, let's say. Ring me here – not at the laboratory."

"I feel fine now," Jonny argued, because he knew Dr Benedicta was being rather tricky. The Rivendell Community number was unlisted, and he had looked in vain under the name Benedicta many times.

"Well, I'm afraid you'll have to wait," she told him firmly. "My dear young man, you're in a terrible state. I'm going to ring your father and ask him to come here and collect you." And she picked up a telephone book that was sitting on the counter.

"I'd rather you didn't," Jonny said. "He wouldn't be very happy about it." His father would be furious all over again at being rung by the Benedictas whom he had never really liked. "He's had one dose of fury already tonight."

"But I don't think he'd be very happy if we left you to find your own way home either," Dr Benedicta said. She was genuinely concerned in spite of being annoyed with him.

"We've had this great discussion of my faults outside the police station," Jonny said. "It went on for ages. I don't think he missed one of them. He won't want to know."

"How did you get here?" asked Dr Ruth. "The last bus went by an hour ago."

"I got a taxi most of the way," said Jonny. "I'll walk back to the city and get another one."

"You won't make it," she told him decisively. "I'm surprised you're still standing. Besides – a taxi – it'll cost you a fortune."

"I've got some money left from the old days," said Jonny, teasing her a little bit. "From when I was rich and famous – a *star*."

"I do remember," said Dr Benedicta dryly.

"There'll be people going back to town in a moment," Jill volunteered from somewhere in the seething kitchen.

"Max is!" cried Amy, and at that moment the door opened and voices shouted from the room beyond, "Ruth! Ruth! Don't miss it."

"Don't miss it!" Jonny echoed, smiling at her. Dr Benedicta stared back at him. She was just as cool and collected as Jonny remembered her, and she was in her own house surrounded by friends. All the same, Jonny saw dimly that he had alarmed her – chaos, come in out of the night where it really belonged, standing and smiling in her well-lighted kitchen. She seized a plastic bucket and placed it at his feet.

"I do want to see the news," she said crisply. "If you even *think* you're going to be sick, for God's sake be sick in the bucket. I don't want to have to clean up after you."

Jonny was left alone in the kitchen. The curtains were not drawn, and he could see his reflection – a dim, dark double, almost featureless, moving as he moved to put on its hat again. The stripes in the old blazer could be distinguished, the yellow patches he himself had neatly sewed on the elbows where the cloth was wearing thin were easy to see. At his neck he caught a metallic gleam as if his head had been severed and the weapon left in the wound, but it just marked the headpiece of his Walkman. All the same his head felt detached. Jonny thought he might close his eyes for a moment and stop struggling against the insistent darkness. Then his eyes fell on the telephone book. Pulling it towards him he opened it at the back, and there, sure enough, on the pages provided, were many numbers and names written down so that they could be located easily. The names darted around the page just ahead of where he was looking, like black wrigglers in a murky pond, but by narrowing his eyes and pinning the words down one at a time with his wavering finger he could hold them still long enough to read them. Halfway down the first column he came on the name *Bonny* and a number and a street address: 115 Marribel Road. Jonny took a pen from a green tumbler full of pens and pencils and, holding his left hand close in front of him as if it were a page and he were a very short-sighted reader, he copied the number and address very slowly and deliberately on to his palm.

Marribel Road. It was a familiar name. He had seen it written up somewhere many times before. At least his journey had not been all in vain.

Jonny relaxed and suddenly felt very tired. There was a burst of sarcastic cheering from next door. He shivered a little. I'll just put my head down... he thought, but the door opened and this time both Dr Benedictas came through followed not only by Polly and Jill, but by a very elegant Maori boy who gave him a scornful look, and a stout man wearing an expensive ski jacket and carrying a flax kitbag full of books. He had thick, floppy, faded hair, and a genial expression.

"...worth doing," the man was saying over his shoulder. "Of course, normally I don't like chanting slogans but..."

"There's nothing much else a crowd of people can do," Bonny's father replied. He was a grey-headed, clever-looking man – craggy, lean and brown as if he went jogging every day. "We were right at the back, and couldn't hear a word the speakers were saying. I'm sure it all made good sense, but I couldn't hear it."

"We'll have to get a better sound system next time," said his wife.

"Hinerangi must have given them a fright," the man with the kitbag went on. "But trust the media to make a big thing out of a simple firecracker. Explosive device, indeed!"

"They can be dangerous, though," said Dr Ruth, frowning. "I do wish she'd done something else. And the police are bound to get her and she'll be in court again."

"Now, where's this young tearaway who needs a lift home?" said the man with the kitbag, turning to look around the kitchen. "Oh, Lord!" he cried when his eyes fell on Jonny. He burst out laughing.

"Borrow the bucket by all means," offered Dr Ruth in a resigned voice. The girls and the dark boy who had begun to make the coffee all cast suspicious glances at him.

"Well, Jonathan," said Bonny's father, "I'm afraid you're going to feel very poorly tomorrow, but it'll pass, won't it, Max?"

"Not in my car, I hope," said Max.

"It's so *bad* for you," exclaimed Dr Ruth. Jonny nodded carefully.

"What did you want to see Bonny about?" her father asked, placing his hand on Jonny's shoulder and gently turning him towards the door.

"It's a secret..." began Jonny, and stopped. ("Because," he was saying eloquently inside his head, "because she once told a lie for me, and I want to be sure why, because sometimes I've got two memories and I can't be sure which is the right one, and she was the witness.")

"It's too complicated to tell," he said aloud, and added, "Well, she knows everything."

Through a flawed glass of memory he saw Bonny and Janine, crouching on either side of a circle of daisy heads, watching intently as Bonny cast the cards with pictures on them up into the air. The cards tumbled back into the circle, and Bonny, ignoring those which were already right-side up, turned one of the others over. "The tower!" he heard her say. "Not again!" said Janine plaintively. Over her shoulder he had seen the card... a tower struck by lightning, its top breaking off, and a figure with hair like pale fire, plunging from the tower to the rocks below.

Bonny's father patted his shoulder.

"Tell me about it," he suggested. "I know everything, too. She gets it from me."

Jonny didn't bother to remind Dr Benedicta that his two daughters were both adopted children. The Benedictas had deliberately adopted children who could never be taken as their own. He folded his fingers protectively over his palm.

"Well, there's one thing no one knows except Bonny and me," he said. "I just wanted to... check up."

"I don't know where the Darts live nowadays," Dr Ruth was saying to Max. "We weren't close friends. It was just that Bonny was so very fond of Janine, this boy's sister." Max must have looked surprised. "I must say Janine was a very bright girl," Dr Ruth added quickly.

"I hope he doesn't live right across town," Max said doubtfully. "It's late at night to be a Good Samaritan."

"Put him off at that taxi rank just where you come off the motorway," Dr Ruth said. "He says he's got plenty of money. Thanks for everything, Max."

"Oh, well," said Max, "we've all been young and silly, haven't we?"

"Not that silly!" said Dr Ruth.

"Not that young!" said the other Dr Benedicta with a sigh.

They were in the yard and had stopped by an old but rather beautiful car – an ancient Alpha Romeo, Jonny saw with some surprise. He looked at Max with a woolly respect. Max was talking across it, taking out his car keys.

"He and his sister used to dance in those dreadful Chickenbits advertisements," Dr Ruth said, just as if Jonny couldn't hear her.

"Oh!" said Max, pausing as he unlocked the door. "Good heavens... *Chick-chick-chick-chick-chicken!* Those ones?"

"Don't remind me," said Dr Ruth.

"I remember them well," said Max from inside the car, still sounding surprised. "You never really think of kids you see like that as being real people, growing up..."

"I'm the only one that did," said Jonny, climbing in at the passenger door. "I won't need the bucket. Tap-dancers have strong stomachs."

"They probably need them!" Dr Ruth remarked, helping him into the car. She sounded rather nasty.

"I've given it up," Jonny said, looking out at her. "I don't dance any more. Never again! Does that make me any better?" He couldn't see her, but when she answered she spoke quite gently.

"Jonathan, I didn't mean…" she began.

"I know what you meant," Jonny told her. "Even drunk, I know. I've always known. OK?" He gave her his brightest television smile and pulled the door shut. Max was struggling to put a seat belt around him.

"I can do it," Jonny said.

"Off we go then!" cried Max. He reversed out into the yard, then swung smoothly into the drive. "Poor Ruth. Bonny's a bit of a recluse these days and it worries her. And then there's all this drama tonight. She's a wonderful woman, Ruth, but she's a worrier."

"She hated tap-dancing," Jonny mumbled. "I think it was all the smiling and sequins." Supported by the safety belt, he felt he could at last surrender a little bit. He was shaking all over. Pushing his hands into his pockets he found first his wallet, then the tapes he carried with him in case silence got too much for him, and finally the present he had planned to give Bonny. He hadn't set out intending to give it to her, but he always carried it with him, and suddenly it had seemed like a good idea. Relaxing, he felt himself spin faster and faster as his head, like a wild centrifuge, flung shred after shred of disintegrating memory into darkness.

CHAPTER TWO

Jonny woke in the night with no idea of place or time, though it was not so much a matter of waking up, as of rising out of an echoless pit. He knew it was night, but thought at first, as he vaguely located hands, head and feet, that he had been sleeping under the influence of moonlight. He found he was lying flat, spread out like the spokes of a wheel, crucified face downwards. "Jonny Dart," his lips murmured to the earth, against which he was pressed, as he remembered his name. "Where am I?" Then he began to go in and out of the old memory which he knew by heart, but which to him was always extraordinary.

Once again Janine fell. For a moment Jonny, seeing her feet leave the ground, had believed she was actually beginning to fly. She had screamed once, just as she went over the edge, but by now the ragged cry of panic was smoothed into a musical tone – the beginning of a new song. It had all been so quick and simple. It was hard to believe it was an accident, for Janine had always danced confidently ahead of him. All his life he had felt himself moved by her left-over grace. Unable to believe what he had seen, he had looked wildly up into the air, seeking confirmation from a higher authority, and there on the path above, safe behind the chain fence and the sign marked 'Danger', stood Bonny Benedicta, wearing her Pythoness clothes, her snake ring, and her jingling necklaces and bracelets – the only other witness to what had happened. All around them the summer evening was perfectly still, the hushed air flooded with clear, golden light.

Bonny was not only Janine's best friend but a story-and-word girl. Even at fourteen, no longer a child, Jonny had never quite escaped the suspicion that things happened because Bonny invented them or foretold them. The game had been going on for years, but at the time of Janine's fall, they only played it ironically, making fun of themselves as children. Perhaps the feeling that it was all over and done with had made Janine careless of the old power, still coiled like a sleeping serpent in the heart of the game, even though it was she who had insisted in the beginning that it had to be really dangerous. Looking up at Bonny, waiting for her to uninvent what had just happened, Jonny couldn't help believing that she would fling her cards into the air, that Janine would rise lightly out of the void and, landing surely on the rocky ledge ahead of him, would go on with the teetering, dangerous dance, challenging gravity on its very frontier.

Janine's fall was not the sort of thing that could be uninvented. After the first terrible jolt, everything had gone on more or less as usual. But, though he had gone along with it, growing and learning, Jonny sometimes felt that his full life had stopped back then. Sometimes he saw himself spreadeagled against that moment, trying to press himself through it so that he could get on with whatever might be on the other side.

"You know what, Dart?" a friend of his had once said with casual acrimony. "Everyone reckons if one of you two had to go over it was a pity it wasn't you." It was no news to Jonny. He had begun believing this while Janine was still spinning in the air.

"Where am I?" he asked himself once more, drifting out of this memory which never left him. At night it was always particularly vivid though remote as well, a dream that it was impossible to wake up from, even after he had opened his eyes.

He ached all over and, touching his face and feeling the outline of a swollen stranger, wondered if he had actually managed, after all, to press himself right through the memory of Janine's fall only to come out on the other side, displaced or even mad. Lying on his back, he stared up through leaves into a sky glazed with unnatural light.

The last thing he remembered with absolute clarity was the sign saying *Rivendell Community*. Going backwards from that, everything was clear enough. He could remember the fight with his father outside the police station. He could remember refusing to get into the car until his father stopped lecturing him, then stalking off while his father called after him, "You'll be back. There's nowhere for you to go."

"You're not a fortune-teller!" Jonny had shouted, walking backwards for a few steps so that he could face his father at the same time as he retreated, then laughing and turning, losing himself in the crowd as quickly as possible.

But on *this* side of the Rivendell sign there was almost nothing in his memory except the sudden appearance of a lighted window, and then a door opening and Dr Ruth Benedicta coming towards him. He had been looking for Bonny with some crazy idea that she might tell him something, but he couldn't remember exactly what he had wanted to be told. He had been offered a lift back to the city and had a memory, surprisingly clear although it was so trivial, of trying to put a seat belt on.

Jonny sat up slowly. He stood, and found that he was standing among bushes on a triangular traffic island, where the motorway, sweeping across a shallow flyover, ended in an asterisk of city streets and came to an end. Across the line of roofs and windows immediately confronting him the word ALPHA, set out in shocking-pink neon, flashed on, flashed off. Jonny knew exactly where he was, for ALPHA was part of the name of a tourist motel on the edge of the city's main shopping centre. Now he began to remember waking up in a strange car, sagging down in the seat belt, remembered getting out and setting off in the general direction of a taxi rank a short distance down one of the intersecting streets. I must have flaked out, he thought with resignation rather than alarm.

The city stretched out around him looking just like the one he had gone to sleep in, but feeling different... Jonny believed, wildly, he had somehow fallen into another place, another time. Feeling terribly ill he tried a step or two, and something moving behind him tugged softly at his belt, but it was only the headphones of his Walkman, fallen off and trailing after him, catching in bushes. Jonny picked up the headphones and frowned at them in the grubby light. He had a vague memory of being sick in these bushes, but the headphones seemed to be perfectly presentable. At last he put them over his head and ears, and then, moved by something almost too instinctive to be called a memory, felt the darkness under the shrubs and found his bandit hat. The tape-recorder unit was still clasped to his belt. Jonny pressed a button. Immediately the night exploded. Music and voices burst wildly in at either ear.

"FEET GONE WANDERING, HEAD'S NO GUIDE, BURN THE WORLD WITH THE FIRE INSIDE."

"What's going on?" he shouted at the city. "What's the secret?"

"GO GO GO TO GONE GONE GONE," sang the band.

Jonny began to jog, deciding to abandon himself to the magic of chance. From now on his signposts would be words overheard accidentally, graffiti, advertisements, street names... and here he paused and looked uncertainly at the backs of his hands. "We work by signs," Bonny had once told him. If he accepted the clues the city offered him, it might point him in the right direction.

"Running away to sea!" he had once overheard Bonny telling Janine. "It really means running away to *see*. See?"

"I'm running away to see!" Jonny said aloud, in time to his footsteps. He had poisoned himself and should be at home in bed, yet here he was, running through empty city streets. In an hour, in ten minutes, any second now, he would begin to feel incapable of movement, would start thinking, What am I doing here? I must be crazy! and would start crawling towards home.

"FROM THE WORLD INTO SILENCE," sang the band.

"Whirled into silence," murmured Bonny's rustling voice. Only the voice was hers, the words were his own. Though she had vanished immediately after Janine died, her echo had gone on working for Jonny, twisting words and sometimes the things they stood for.

Jonny took the least familiar street, one beginning with large, well-kept shops and lighted windows, but decaying into other smaller, meaner shops more in keeping with

Jonny's own feeling of being exhausted, shabby, dirty and sick. Waves of sickness swept over him, and sometimes he had to stop and lean his forehead against the cool glass of the nearest shop window until the wave had roared in his ears and passed over him.

Bonny had been Janine's best friend, a friend so close that even when the Darts moved to Colville, an inner-city suburb, they insisted on remaining friends, visiting each other after school, and spending weekends at one another's houses. Jonny had been nine, a new pupil in a new school, at a time when his appearance in a television commercial made him terribly easy to recognise. His first friends had been left behind on the other side of town, and for nearly a year his after-school playing time had been spent tagging along after the older girls, backwards and forwards across a hilly, municipal park – Seacliff Heights Reserve – overlooking the sea. If Bonny was the Pythoness, the namer and the storyteller, Janine was the one who had turned the whole Reserve into a stage over which they acted a series of adventures.

The first test was always the same. Climbing past the danger sign under the chain fence that marked the path, they would scramble down on to a narrow, rocky ledge, not unlike the ridgepole of a roof. Below the ledge, a steep, crumbling slope swooped to abrupt cliffs – then nothing but sky and the backs of gulls, and the sea constantly fretting and complaining on the rocks far below. Once the ridge had been negotiated, their rituals began. Certain trees were climbed – always in a particular order and in a particular way. They swung over the creek on a rope which they had tied to the branch of a big willow. They had passwords and spells and secret names for one another.

The sickness retreated a little. Jonny walked on, still hearing the sea. In the light of the city he could almost make out the colours of his old blazer, bought at a church stall in the town square. Though the red looked black, the black looked even blacker, and the yellow was a lurid ghost of itself. His wallet was still safe – not that there was much that anyone could have stolen from it. Though he had told Dr Ruth Benedicta that he had plenty of money, in fact he had none at all – at least nothing on him. His wallet held his post-office savings book, the card from a record club, and very little else besides. In the top pocket of his blazer he had nothing but a comb.

Jonny had yearned to be like Janine and Bonny, to have another secret self, something fierce and wild and full of uncontrollable power, as different as possible from the way he was in real life ("What *are* you?" his fearsome enemies at school shouted at him savagely. They were not really asking him anything, and anyway he had no answer to give them). In the game with Janine and Bonny he demanded to be known as the Wolfman.

The girls had deliberated, watching him secretly through the strands of their untidy hair, Janine's as pale as thistledown, Bonny's the yellowish brown of certain honeysuckle flowers. Her skin matched her hair. He had never known anyone who looked so much the same colour all over, but it was because she had what his mother called "mixed blood". Mrs Dart could never quite understand why the Benedictas should adopt children who so obviously did not belong to them.

"Go and play with your own friends," Janine had told Jonny impatiently and perhaps a little cruelly, for she knew that, at that particular time, he didn't have any.

"Consult the cards!" Bonny had cried, and they had gathered around while she tossed them up into the air. "Look!" she said. "The moon! That means he can be the Wolfman.

He can have a forest of his own,

In which to wander, howl and groan.'"

The Pythoness had always sounded to Jonny like a giant snake, but Bonny said she was a priestess who told fortunes in rhyme.

"Your forest will go wherever you go," she told him. "But it will only become visible at full moon." She mumbled to herself and looked at the sky.

"'In the moon's full silver hour,

You shall be the wolf of power,'"

she had promised him, at last.

"ONCE IN THE OLD DAYS..." the band sang savagely in his ear as Jonny came out into another road, where, overcome once more by the poison in his blood, he had to sit down and put his head on his knees.

A night wind, patrolling the city, rushed at him, its paws on his chest, slapping his face with an icy tongue. Jonny, revived, got to his feet and pushed against it out into the main road opposite yet another intersection. Street lights looked down at him from long, slender necks of concrete, curving over at the top as if light were too great a burden to be held. Factory fronts were illuminated. Fences warned that they were protected by electronic devices, security services or guard dogs. Fingered by light, Jonny felt small and strange and desolate. The wind idly stirred rubbish in the gutter. Brittle paper twitched, scuttled, grew still. Jonny watched it, then lifted his eyes to the street sign and nodded as if, somehow, he had expected to find himself there, the only man in an insubstantial world. He crossed the road and set off down the opposite street which was lined with buildings, loading bays, fences of steel pipe and wire mesh. A beach or a hillside might be deserted and still seem completely itself, but an industrial street depended on cars and people. Without them it became both eerie and pathetic, its true function lost until morning. The music ended, but Jonny did not bother to change the tape. He simply pushed the headphones back from his head. He'd heard enough messages for the moment.

Suddenly the walls stopped. Jonny had come upon a huge open car park, attached to a shopping complex and dominated by a large supermarket. Feeling like a man from outer-space revisiting the world after the neutron bomb had killed every living thing but left all property intact, he hesitated. He was unwilling to commit himself to that wide, empty space and to be revealed as the only living thing in a dead city. Traffic lights, just a little ahead, changed colour. To his surprise in this early morning silence he heard the clockwork of their change.

WALK! the city instructed him. Jonny launched himself across the sterile plain. Nearly halfway across he thought he saw a movement and looked anxiously sideways. The shop windows were reflecting his progress, not in any detail, simply as a black convulsion in the glass. Jonny watched the tremble out of the corner of his eye, though he was moving further and further away from the shopping frontage.

Suddenly, with childish horror, he saw another movement in the glass. Something rippled towards him. Incredibly, the stone desert had disgorged another inhabitant. Jonny and the other person were bound to meet in the centre of the empty car park in the grimy light of the empty city. He turned his head. A stunted person in a long coat was pushing a supermarket trolley along the opposite diagonal to the one he was taking. A moment later he made out a short, thin, old woman wearing a hat like a crimson chamber-pot without a handle. Strands of grey hair hung around her ears. He thought he must look equally strange to her in his striped blazer, bloodstained shirt and blue jeans, his face swollen under his fringe of brown curls. Yet she smiled as she came towards him as if he were the very one she had been waiting for.

He altered his direction slightly so that it would be easy for her to avoid him, but then she altered hers, pushing the trolley at him as if she intended to knock him over with it – to scoop him up and carry him off. The city was aiming them at one another, or so Jonny half-believed. He was relieved to find he did not recognise the old woman. A hundred years might have gone by while he slept on the traffic island and now perhaps he was about to meet his mother or even one of the twins, screwed up by time. He could make out deep wrinkles and a smile; the eyes were invisible under the pot hat.

He hesitated and stood completely still so that the old lady could walk past him, but instead she came right up to him, staring at him, smiling, as if she were waiting for him to begin a conversation. Jonny remained silent. In the end she was the one who spoke first.

"Are *you* the one?" she asked. Her voice was old but distinct, crisp, cultured – a voice from Benedicta country. "Are *you* the one?" she asked again.

"I don't know," Jonny said. After a moment he added, "My name's Jonathan Dart." He felt he had puzzled her.

"I didn't know you'd changed your name," she remarked easily, and then suddenly became rather bossy and imperious. "Well, I'm not hanging around here all night." She looked around her. "No one's going to impose on *me*," she added, frowning and nodding with mysterious significance, moving off a few steps before turning once more.

"Are you coming, or aren't you?" she asked him. "I don't know about you but I could do with a nice cup of tea. It's no good going to the shops. They're all shut! I think it must be Sunday." She moved another few steps. "Are you coming?" she asked.

A white van, the first vehicle Jonny had seen in all his night wanderings, roared past. It sounded as if the exhaust pipe were missing. Someone shouted and lobbed a can out from the darkness in the cab. It bounced once... twice. As the sound of the engine died away, the tinny trickle of the can, still rolling, made itself heard, carrying a tiny echo with it that amplified it strangely. The mere thought of beer made Jonny want to be sick, and the degrading picture of himself being sick in front of anyone, and in a public place, was barely enough to save him. He recovered, but the can was still rolling. There must have been a little slope in the apparently flat car park.

I'll walk her to the corner, thought Jonny. Just to make sure she's safe. But as he walked after her like an obedient dog, he was filled with a credulous enchantment.

"What's your name, anyway?" he asked her, being deliberately offhand and disrespectful so that she would know he wasn't really under her control. "I've told you mine."

"It's still the same," she said, sounding surprised. "You only change one when you get married."

"Give me a clue," Jonny suggested, padding along beside her.

"Sophie!" she cried. "I'm the angel of wisdom. Remember the good old days!"

"Go on!" said Jonny after a pause. "Gosh, I'm glad to meet you at last. You could be a big help to me."

But she smiled as if she knew they were already old friends and, pushing the empty trolley, led him out of the car park and into a one-way street.

CHAPTER THREE

As they went out of the car park, Jonny could not be certain if he was in charge of this old night creature or if she was in charge of him. But then it was half-past three in the morning, and at such an hour shops and offices existed for their own incomprehensible reasons, and there was no sure proof of human existence any more.

Plastic Fabrications said a narrow sign on a brick wall, which might have been a clue. *Barry loves Carmen* someone had written on the footpath, surrounding the information with a fuzzy heart painted with red spray. Jonny, the Crusoe of the traffic island, had found himself a singular Friday.

Friday, Jonny thought suddenly. I've got to appear in the District Court on Friday.

It was not good news but he was pleased to reclaim anything from the oblivion of the last few hours. *Cognito Systems* a silvery notice announced elegantly. *Marribel Road* said another in a more commonplace style. The street name, like all city street names, was painted black on white, and fastened to a telegraph pole. Jonny stopped and stared at this name, frowning and startled. Memory had flashed at him, but its sudden pulse, densely packed with information, had gone right through him, taking everything with it into darkness on the other side. His companion, now several paces ahead of him, stopped and looked back at him, apparently puzzled and impatient. Jonny continued to stare up at the street sign which tantalised him with promises he could not remember. However, for the present at least, it kept its secrets. At last he gave up and, like a man bound by enchantment, he began to follow his eerie guide once more.

They walked for three blocks down Marribel Road, past three lots of traffic lights all clicking away, flashing instructions to non-existent traffic. His companion, however, insisted on stopping at every red light, even though Marribel Road, stretching forward and back as far as the eye could see, did not contain a single pair of headlights to watch out for. White arrows painted on the sealed surface indicated that it was a one-way street, but there was nothing moving in either direction. At the third set of traffic lights they found themselves in an old shopping centre, shabbier than the one they had left three blocks behind them. Some shops were empty, glass broken, windows boarded over. There was a post office on one corner and a pub diagonally opposite it.

The Colville, Jonny read, and stopped short for a second time, electrified by memory. All this time he had believed he was offering himself blindly to chance. His feet, independent and treacherous, had been purposefully dancing him back to scenes of torment. Perhaps that was why the name Marribel Road had seemed so unexpectedly important. It must have been a warning he had failed to recognise. For, not far from this very spot, he had been forced to tap-dance in the boys' toilet at school. He remembered, far more vividly than he wished to, his particular oppressor, Nev Fowler, seizing him by the collar, pushing his head of newly bleached hair into a bowl and flushing water all over it. He remembered other more frightening things for, once out of school, Nev Fowler had hung a knife at his belt and had threatened to kill him. For nearly a year Jonny had really believed that Nev was planning to cut his throat, and was just waiting for the right, lonely occasion. At home he did not dare suggest that tap-dancing in a television advertisement was bringing him close to death.

"First step on the way to stardom!" Mrs Dart had been saying. She was delighted with the exciting work the agency had found for Jonny and Janine, thrilled not only with the money but with the prospect of stardom, which seemed like a sort of immortality.

Sophie had stopped outside the post office and was looking at it in a puzzled way.

"I could take some money out," she suggested uncertainly. "I don't like to run short."

"No. You're short enough already," Jonny agreed, and felt better, dissolving ghosts with a thin joke. "It's shut. Come back tomorrow." They walked past the post office, their shadows stretching silently ahead, then sliding beside them, then lagging behind – lengthening and shortening as one street light took over from another. There was a new building, *Integrity Electronics,* and then a railway line. With dull amazement Jonny saw another empty supermarket trolley sitting beside the line, strange and glittering on the rough gravel.

"I'm not taking this one any further," Sophie announced, giving Jonny a defiant stare, apparently expecting him to protest, but he shrugged carelessly as she parked it neatly beside the other one.

"They can't shoulder me with all that responsibility," she added in a confiding voice, nodding at him significantly.

"Who's they?" Jonny asked.

"The people next door," she muttered, giving him as sinister a look from under her narrow, crimson hat brim as any he gave from under his black one. The footpath had stopped. They walked over a strip of gravel, then crossed the railway line, though not without difficulty. Sophie's feet, in their flat, black shoes, felt their way uneasily over the uneven surfaces of iron and wood and loose stones. Even though he was feeling ill, Jonny was sure-footed. He always had been.

He had actually enjoyed tap-dancing. Nothing could quite alter that. When he danced, just every now and then, Jonny believed he was set free from gravity. The actual dancing was a public thing, but the feeling was a private one. His feet touched the ground, not because they had to, but simply because they needed it to mark out a complex rhythm. Every now and then he moved beyond being Jonathan Dart, beyond being the Chickenbits boy, as rhythm itself, looking for a way of becoming visible, chose to possess him and make him its outward sign. Being projected in living colour into thousands of homes every evening was nothing to do with feelings such as these. It was just bad luck that one of the homes had been Nev Fowler's.

On the other side of the track the footpath began again. Jonny and Sophie passed a high fence with a few boards missing – a car-wrecker's yard, completely overgrown in parts. Shapes of old cars, agonised and partly dismembered, reared out of the grass and weeds.

How much further? wondered Jonny. For the first time it occurred to him that his companion might not actually know where she was going. He imagined some family driving up to the supermarket, sliding their granny out like an unwanted cat and driving furtively off again. He himself had once adopted a little cat that had been discarded in this way, but now it loved his mother best. His bruised face felt like a mask. He'd have to decide just what expression he would need most in the next twenty-four hours, since any attempt to alter it might cause the mask to crack and crumble away. In a moment his whole face would be gone, leaving him with only raw meat and nerve ends to turn towards the world.

The journey's end was in sight. Beyond the wrecker's yard there were two old houses standing side by side: tall, thin, twin houses, belonging to the early part of the century – come down in the world but still respectable.

Jonny looked at the first one with astonishment. From between its top windows there protruded a huge, old-fashioned tap, painted purple. A tap like that, turned on and forgotten, could flood the whole city. Even if you left it dripping it would be serious. Each drop would hold about two gallons of water at least. Directly below the tap was a small, cramped balcony with two more windows giving on to it – one lit, the other darkened in a cunning wink.

I know, but I'm not telling, the house was saying to him. A strong yellow glow leaked out around skimpy curtains, spilling over the balcony. Its shadow across their path was so black it could have been a hole, leading down between cellars and foundations to the water-mains and sewers which flow under any city. At street level Tap House had a garage door that looked as if it hadn't been opened for ages.

ARE YOU THE PERSON GOD WANTS YOU TO BE? someone had painted on the garage door, but someone else had put a line with a blue spray can through the word 'person' and substituted the word 'sheep'. By adding a protest of their own, it now read, ARE YOU THE SHEEP GOD WANTS YOU TO BE? NO LIVE SHEEP EXPORTS TO IRAN! News stalked you all the way round the city, Jonny thought. Everyone was twitchy about something, and needed to tell about it. Beyond this garage door was another door, equally secretive, but with no lettering on it, fitting tightly into its doorway, no door handle, only a Yale lock. There was a small, rickety letterbox fastened to the wall beside this door, while between the two doors and just under the balcony was a long sign, lying flat along the wall:

TAP HOUSE

ERROL WEST: MASTER PLUMBER

Plumbing installations and services

The house next door had no signs painted on it, but vandals had split its letterbox in half. It hung askew on its bolts, its wounded top driven into a shallow V – definitely a dead letterbox, Jonny thought, looking at it uneasily. All the same, someone must get letters delivered there. There was a clean milk bottle on the front step.

Sophie had begun sorting through her handbag which appeared to be entirely filled with small purses, tissues, envelopes that had to be peered into and pockets that had to be unzipped. She pushed her knobbly fingers into one crevice after another, giving small exclamations of impatience and distress.

"I know I took the key with me," she said at last. "You haven't got it, have you?"

"Look: no key!" Jonny said, holding his hands up, fingers spread.

"I wonder if those people next door..." she began, and wheeled around to stare at the next-door house very suspiciously. Apparently responding to her stare, a light came on. Jonny grinned.

"They know you're after them," he said. "Have you tried your coat pockets?"

"Oh, no!" Sophie said. "I never put keys there." Her voice, solemn and concerned to begin with, suddenly grew more and more light-hearted as she went on. "I always keep them on this string around my neck," and, without any hesitation, she pulled out of the flat bosom of her plastic raincoat a long loop of string jangling with several keys.

"My memory's not as good as it could be," she confided to Jonny, holding the string up to the light, squinting at the keys. "But I always keep them there because if I mislaid them, well, anyone could find them, and just walk in off the streets. Anyone!"

"Anyone could," Jonny agreed, and though it was not full moon, there was a bit of the Wolfman in his careful smile.

Sophie chose a key that certainly looked possible. She tried it; it fitted. She turned it. The door swung open, and he saw a tiny entrance hall, coats hanging on coathooks, and the bottom steps of a staircase skirted by a passage to the back of the house. Everything was cramped – all the more so because, under the coathooks, sat a supermarket trolley filled with shoes.

"We left one of those back by the railway line," he commented.

"Yes, we don't need two," she said in a practical voice, and added, "they don't always put one out, you know." Then she went into Tap House. Jonny hesitated. If he went in after her, Wolfman or not, he might never come out again. He imagined some owner of Tap House opening a wardrobe door in the distant future and finding Jonny Dart hanging from one of the coathooks, dried out, leathery, but still recognisable.

"Are you going to stay out there all night?" Sophie asked, shaking the door slightly. Jonny still hesitated, shifting from one foot to the other, for, house of doom or not, he longed to be somewhere he could sit down. He did not dare let himself begin thinking that it would be wonderful to *lie* down. As he looked around, half hoping for instruction out of the air, he saw that he was being observed from the balcony next door. The light from inside, weak though it was, suggested a figure standing back in the shadows, a vague, inhuman outline. Jonny had the impression of a head, elongated and completely bald. Startled by the thought of aliens, he stepped rapidly over the threshold and Sophie closed the door behind him.

The smell was indescribable. It drove everything else out of his head. His nose tried to close itself in outrage and he began to breathe through his mouth, taking in as little air as he could and getting rid of it as quickly as possible. The staircase, rising up into darkness, was alive with movement, soft, running footsteps, faint rustlings, the sound of a small population in retreat. Several people were at war somewhere in his head – a good-hearted boy who had once been a Scout and wanted to see an old lady safely home; the mad, searching Wolfman, expecting the city to guide him with magical clues even though he was not sure what he was searching for; and then a third man, overlapping both the other two, but on the whole more real than either of them, who might suddenly take over and say, "For God's sake, what *am* I doing *here*? How did I get *into* this? How do I get *out*?"

These thoughts were complicated by the realisation that he was no longer feeling vaguely seedy, but was going to be very sick quite soon. He needed to make quick arrangements. Trying to swallow at the same time as he was breathing, he followed Sophie up her narrow stairs to a tiny landing lit by a single, naked light bulb which shone with a dreary, brownish light. Here the old stair, which had looked as if it were going to peter out, turned at an angle and led on upwards, but Sophie opened the nearer of the two doors that marked her landing and went through it.

Jonny meekly followed. For half a breath the room beyond held together. Then its whole surface burst violently apart. It was full of cats, more cats than he had ever seen collected in one place. Horrified at the sight of a stranger, they fled through two open doorways, except for one cat which remained flattened defensively on the hearthrug and one which stayed curled in its chair, barely moving.

"Puss, puss!" said Jonny in a high, weak voice. Slowly the hearthrug-cat decided that it was not in danger and relaxed a little, though still watching Jonny intently. The cat in the chair did not stir. The green crescent of a half-closed eye looked out from the safe, firm curve of the body, latched around with its own fine tail. Jonny wished he could curl up like that, be self-contained, make himself into a circle, his own beginning and end.

"Sophie," he began in a strained voice. There was a revolting smell in the room, coarse, with a chemical edge, suggesting that rubber had been burned there recently along with contributions from the cats. "Sophie," he said, gagging slightly, "where's the toilet? I need it quickly."

Sophie turned and stared at him accusingly.

"Nana wouldn't have liked to hear you say 'toilet'," she said maddeningly. "'Lavatory' is the proper word."

"Where is it?" Jonny demanded through clenched teeth. He wanted to shout at her but felt it was too dangerous.

"Let me see..." began Sophie very slowly, staring reflectively around her. Swallowing desperately, Jonny dashed to one of the open doors. The light was on, showing a bed with the blankets strained over it sideways, and an inscrutable square lump covered in a sort of turquoise fur. Turning, he scrambled back across the room on to the landing, opened a second door, and discovered, to his huge relief, a chipped bath standing tall on clawed feet, a massive hand-basin and a big, old-fashioned lavatory with a high overhead tank and a piece of frayed rope hanging down from it. Jonny barely made it. From behind the bath a striped cat watched him with understandable revulsion.

As his outraged stomach relaxed at last and he sat back on his heels, the cat leaped gracefully on to the hand-basin, stared fixedly upward, working its hindlegs nervously up and down, then launched itself high into the air, landing on the overhead tank from which it moved into a small square opening that had once been filled with slats of glass. Once there it turned, looked disdainfully down at him, twitched its tail and vanished, landing, from the sound of it, on an expanse of tin somewhere out in the night.

Jonny rose to his feet, trembling and exhausted, but purified. He felt a religious certainty that he would never get drunk again. He saw himself in the future – a jovial, good fellow, still one of the boys, but smiling and placing his hand over the glass when beer or wine were offered – nothing self-righteous, just a quiet refusal. He would only drink wholesome fruit juice from now on.

How wonderful modern drainage was! His sins would be washed away. He tugged the frayed rope but nothing happened. He tugged harder, and a prolonged creaking and complaining began overhead. The whole system choked and struggled. Its problems were much worse than his. He began to feel guilty for burdening it beyond its capacity. The whole bathroom shuddered as he tugged the rope violently, but he was rewarded at last with an angry, efficient flow that roared and hiccuped and roared again.

Jonny sighed with relief, washed his hands carefully, rather disconcerted to find that what looked like a cake of cracked, yellow soap was actually a small block of cheese set squarely in the soap-dish. A small nail brush with grey, bent bristles caught his eye and he scrubbed his hands vigorously. There was no towel, though various dirty rags were hung very tidily along the edge of the bath. At this point, trying to shake his hands dry, Jonny suddenly saw a faint inscription in the palm of his left hand. He tried to read it, but the limp scrubbing brush had been surprisingly effective. After staring at wet skin for several seconds, Jonny held his hand up in the air, closer to the light. *Marribel Road,* he made out incredulously – but all else was gone. Then, before he had time to think about this in any detail, something began screaming in the other room – a shrill, horrifying cry. Jonny's first thought was that his hostess must be grilling a cat for supper, but the cry went on and on, getting higher and higher. Whatever it was that was doing the crying did not need to breathe. He went to investigate.

The screaming came from a kettle sitting on a red-hot ring. Steam came from it in puffs that reminded Jonny of comic-book speech balloons.

The old woman was in the kitchen, beside the window that had looked on to the balcony.

Sophie was frantically looking for the source of the scream in a cupboard under the sink. Jonny reached over her, took the kettle off the ring, and stood it on top of a small fridge. Two lines of tin-foil tops from milk bottles were set out in a careful order just as if Sophie were proposing to play a game with them.

The paw marks of cats were everywhere. On the kitchen counter was a pink receipt of some kind. *Twelve dollars,* it read, signed, *Spike.* Jonny read it automatically. It was right under his eye.

"Cup of tea, Sophie?" he asked. After all, the water had boiled.

"I'll have one for you in a moment," she cried happily. "I remember just how you like it." And she beamed at him with such uncritical kindness that he felt, for the first time, the nudge of a feeling which was not curiosity or superstition or pity or distaste. He could not name it, but it wrenched at him as if *he* were the old one, damaged beyond all mending, and she was the innocent, dangerously adrift in a savage night-world.

"Oh, there it is!" she cried, pouncing on her handbag, rather as if she were thinking of making tea in it. Then she stood holding it and looking at it in a puzzled way, knowing something was not quite right.

"You need a teapot," Jonny suggested quickly.

The teapot was ready to hand. The canister beside it was marked *Tea* but it was empty. Jonny turned, and experimentally opened a cupboard. No less than seven packets of biscuits made a sudden rush for freedom. Sophie was displeased.

"Those are my thingummies," she said, and paused, searching for the right word. She hunted through a private jumble of possibilities without success. "Out you go!" she said at last, benevolently but firmly getting him out of her way. "Just sit down and relax, and *I'll* bring it."

Stepping out over an archipelago of cats' saucers, some filled with sour milk and one with sliced banana, Jonny left her to it. He longed for sleep, real sleep, not unconsciousness, but could not imagine how he might get any.

The carpet in the sitting room was reasonably new, though badly in need of being vacuumed or swept. There was a little table and four chairs made of chrome and vinyl, a large settee that looked as if it had been upholstered in a primitive green tartan, and an armchair richly laced with cat hair. Standing back against one wall was a little desk, its lid open on a series of orderly pigeon holes. From where he stood Jonny could see a banana skin in one of them, and a roll of lavatory paper – something the bathroom had lacked – in another. On the wall were two pictures, one of ducks landing on a lake, wings up, feet down, black against a lurid sunset, and another of horses running wild across a vast plain. Leaving this room, Jonny explored the dog-leg stair and, climbing, found another landing and two big rooms on the next level – the original bedrooms of the house, since the room where Sophie apparently slept had almost certainly been intended as a breakfast room. In one of the top rooms was a double bed with a mattress, a pillow and four faded blankets folded at the end of it. Downstairs the kettle screamed briefly, but this time it was silenced at once. In spite of cats and smells and cheese in the soap-dish, the bed looked wonderfully inviting.

What on earth am I doing, checking the place out like this? Jonny thought with dismay. Anyone would think I was planning to stay here. But, after all, he had nowhere else to go.

"Are you there?" Sophie called up from the landing in her crisp, elegant, old voice, and then added a name that was not his own, a name he couldn't quite catch.

When Jonny went downstairs, he found she had set the little table with about five cups and saucers and had dressed the teapot in a bulky, stained, patchwork tea-cosy topped by a doll with a broken face.

"Now for the cakes!" she announced joyously, vanishing and then returning with a big, chipped, enamel dish on which were unopened packets of biscuits and half a chocolate cake, still in its cellophane wrapper. Jonny was becoming more resigned to the smell, and felt a sort of exhausted pleasure in this mad tea party. This was the hidden machinery of life, not a clean, clinical well-oiled engine, monitored by a thousand meticulous dials, but a crazy, stumbling contraption made up of strange things roughly fitted together – things like a huge tap, a dog-leg stair, cheese in the soap-dish and a crocheted tea-cosy stiff with dirt and topped by a doll's broken face. Jonny had always been aware of this limping machine, even under the clean, smooth surface of his own home. Now it had materialised before him. Sophie sat down rather primly and faced Jonny across the teapot.

"Just because you're here," she began astoundingly, "don't think you can..." she paused, "get *up* to anything," she finally said. Jonny's mouth fell open. "You never know where that sort of thing will end," she told him.

"OK," Jonny replied, when he was able. "I respect your principles."

She smiled approvingly and tilted the pot towards the cup nearest to him. A crystal arc curved vigorously from the brown spout. She filled two cups with water quite untainted by tea. Jonny accepted his with relief rather than disappointment, but Sophie sat peering into her own cup, aware that something was not quite right.

"It's very weak," she said dubiously.

"I like it like this," Jonny replied, opening the packet of biscuits which Sophie eyed greedily for a moment before glancing back at her cup of water and resuming her dissatisfied expression. Peeping down into it, like some gypsy studying a prophetic crystal, a Pytheness on a small scale, she sighed deeply, and at last added milk, clouding it and concealing all prophesies for ever. Then her spotted, knotted old hands, little finger crooked daintily, brought a huge milk jug imperiously down on Jonny's cup.

"Not thanks – not for me!" said Jonny hastily. "I don't take any."

Sophie was satisfied with this. Indeed her face lit up.

"Quite right!" she agreed. "I was reading a piece in the paper yesterday, or only the day before, saying that dairy produce was bad for us. I cut it out and kept it, because it's interesting, a thing like that. Remember in the old days when we had to drink a mug of milk with every meal, but now they say it can give you all sorts of troubles. Dairy produce, refined sugars, even eggs – all bad for you!" She began to eat a biscuit, holding it delicately, eating as if biting and chewing were somehow improper and had to be done invisibly. Crumbs made a tiny sound falling on her plastic raincoat. It suddenly occurred to Jonny that she might actually be hungry. In between discreet mouthfuls of her biscuit she talked politely, and mistakenly, about the day's weather and the progress of the season. She referred to people Jonny did not know as if they were old friends of his, and he sat there listening rather apathetically, almost too tired to move.

"Sophie," he said at last, "do you mind if I go upstairs and crash?" She looked at him, dismayed. "I mean, go to sleep. I'm really tired."

"You must do as you see fit," she said graciously, and then as if he had given her a signal to do so, carefully removed her hat revealing a wide, square, freckled forehead almost devoid of eyebrows, crushed locks of stringy, sparse white hair with a crooked pink parting. What he had taken to be an olive complexion was simply a dirty one, but he had already realised that part of the strong atmosphere of the house was Sophie's own personal smell. For the second time that evening he was aware of the wrench of a feeling he was unable to name, except that it had both sadness and rebellion in it.

"I'll rinse my dishes first," he said, picking up his cup and saucer, and going through to the kitchen.

"I'll do mine, too," Sophie said eagerly. "I always think that it's so much nicer in the morning if you clean up the night before."

"Isn't that the Lord's truth," Jonny said. The first relief over, he was beginning to feel sick and clammy again.

Head and stomach were ganging up on him. Did I drink anything at the Benedictas'? he wondered uneasily, dimly remembering a glass in someone's hand at some stage, but not sure if the hand was his. He was sure he had never felt as ill in his life before.

In the kitchen, stepping among the cats' dishes, he noticed a cutting from a paper pasted to the wall. It was brown with age, and a date (seven years earlier) was written on it by hand. *Dieticians Disagree over Value of Dairy Products,* said the heading. Beside him, Sophie searched vainly for tea-towels. She stood in one of the cats' saucers and broke it, but the milk was too thick to run. Looking down at it helplessly, she announced that she was going to bed.

"I'm locking my door," she said, significantly. "I know you mean well, but there is that weakness in the Babbitts. Uncle Brian!" she added with heavy significance, pulling a little face.

Jonny began to reassure her, but she held up her hand with the air of one who would hear no argument. "I know nobody felt Errol was quite – well – quite in our class," she said, tightening her lips slightly, "but he was a dear man and never once lifted his hand to me. Now Eva's husband was a Courtenay, but I happen to know he struck her on several occasions."

"Someone said women should be struck regularly, like gongs," Jonny pointed out, teasing her a little. "I think it was Noel Coward. Some star, anyway."

"Oh, I don't think that can be right," Sophie replied, looking worried. "My father would never have struck my mother and he was an MA."

"Oh, well, there you are then," said Jonny. "Anyhow, you're right. I can't be very reliable or I wouldn't be here."

"You always *meant* well," she said. "I do understand that."

"Mostly I do," Jonny said in surprise. "Only it's not enough."

She gave him a very sweet smile. "It's lovely to have you here. There's no one quite like one of your own, is there!"

Jonny heard her door shut firmly, and then a curious dragging sound. He concluded she was barricading herself in.

Going to the bathroom he was violently sick once more. Then he brushed his teeth as well as he could with his finger and gave himself a symbolic wash with his handkerchief. He studied his palm once more, certain that something important was escaping him, but there was nothing more to be understood from it. So he climbed the stairs to the bedroom, put his Walkman on the top of the chest of drawers, piling the tapes beside it. The curtains were wide open, and as he went over to pull them shut he found himself looking across some sort of a wall at another wall beyond, and there he saw an indistinct shadow-show, two people facing one another, and began to hear the sound of voices.

Though he could not hear the words, he could recognise the staccato beat of an argument. He watched for a second as the shadow puppets gesticulated in time to their words, each conducting a different tune. It was fascinating, but Jonny's evening had held too much fascination already. Even if he had seen murder done he might not have been able to do anything more resourceful than go to bed. As it was he simply pulled the curtains shut, then, carefully hanging his blazer on the door handle, he stripped himself naked, rolled himself in the rugs and toppled into bed. The fight in the pub, the arguments outside the police station, Dr Ruth Benedicta, the journey through the night-time city all ran fast-forward behind his closed lids, accompanied by music which had no location, but simply came out of the air quite close to his ear as if the pillow were singing wordlessly. Jonny thought he listened for a long time, but really it was gone almost as soon as he heard it, crowded out of his head by a sleep of profound exhaustion.

CHAPTER FOUR

Waking for the second time that morning Jonny believed that he had found his way back to the sea. Somewhere at the bottom of the cliffs the air roared, idled, and then roared again, and in the moment between sleeping and waking, the needle jumped on the scratched record. Janine screamed and flapped like a crippled seabird and tried to fly. People often close their eyes on what they do not want to see, but Jonny opened his as wide as he could.

"OUT OF THE WILD BLUE," sang the band, although the headphones lay like a collapsed alien skull on the painted chest of drawers. Above him, a strange ceiling; around him a strange room... He sat up slowly, blinking and groaning. The receding night was troubling but insubstantial, like a complicated nightmare, but it had happened. It could not be slept away. He did not know whether to be dismayed or grateful that his memory, like that of an erratic computer, had swallowed whole great pieces of itself. Of course the sound outside was not the sea. It lacked the sad, timeless murmur of the sea. All the same it triggered familiar images, moving according to a clockwork that was five years old.

Everything at the edge of the cliff had been so strong, so still, so serene, so empty. But then, poised precariously as he was among frail bushes, bending wildly over the abyss, he had made out a scarlet rag far below, fluttering in the shallow tidal breath of the sea. It was Janine's red dress, wound around with pale, disintegrating snakes of sea foam. For one blinding moment Jonny's legs had tensed under him. She might still be saved by a magic act – a sacrifice.

"Jonny," called Bonny from behind the danger sign. "Don't look! Don't jump!" Wearing her snake ring she had been able to read his thoughts. In the next moment, though he still believed that there had been a mistake and that he should be the one to be lying below among the serpents of foam, he also understood that, even if he did throw himself after her, nothing would be changed. Janine would not rise again. He began to scramble back up the slope, the rotten rock rattling away under his hands and feet as he climbed.

However, the tension of that unfulfilled jump was still coiled up in him and some day, on some other occasion, he might set it free. Lying in bed in Sophie's house, he found he had woken with his legs drawn up, his breath drawn in, his shoulders strained forward with that old, instinctive intention.

Jonny knew he had somehow wound up in a house empty of the right things, filled with the wrong ones, where a mad queen ruled over a wild, whiskered, slinking tribe. His head, overloaded with memories, had been naturally drawn to a memory vacuum, but he realised he must get out at once – get out and find his way home before he forgot the way, apologise to his mother, even to his father. Last night he had gone after something in a wild night-chase, tried to catch it, name it and make it his. Transformed by drink and violence, he had somehow transformed everything around him. Now, however, he had woken up, safely back in the world of common sense, and whatever it was – whatever it had been – had hidden itself away until next time.

Of course, it would be a while before he felt properly cured from such overdoses of drink and destiny. Never again, Jonny promised himself. I'll never drink again, I'll even turn herbal and vegetarian, too. Dressing, he fastened the cassette player at his waist, hooked the headphones around his neck and put on his bandit hat. Then he opened the door and went swiftly down the first part of the dog-leg stair, heading firmly towards a better life.

But as he came on to the landing he found old Sophie, sensational in a strange collection of underwear, rising up the stairs towards him with a bottle of milk in her hand. They stopped at the sight of each other, Jonny embarrassed, Sophie outraged.

"How did *you* get in?" she demanded.

"*You* let me in," Jonny said. "Don't you remember? You picked me up last night."

"I did *not*," she said icily, tightening her lips, then turning them down like a cross mouth in a child's drawing.

"Sorry," said Jonny placatingly. "OK – blame me! I shouldn't go home with strange women."

He was irritated to find he was rather hurt by her rejection. However, even as he began to understand she was being cross in order to hide her fear, her expression changed.

"How did you get in?" she asked him once more, but this time the question sounded happy and excited. "It's lovely to see you again," she added fervently. "After all these years, suddenly there you are!" Her face twitched, her mouth relaxed and for a moment he thought she was about to weep. "Come into the comfortable room and I'll make you a cup of tea in next to no time."

"To tell you the truth," Jonny began uneasily, "I actually thought – well, I should be on my way..." but her expression became one of such ludicrous disappointment that he grew silent.

"You've only just come!" she cried. "I could make you a nice little lunch with some of those whatsitsnames."

Jonny looked at his watch. Nine thirty-eight in the morning. His mother would probably be imagining him safe in a flat occupied by four disreputable but familiar friends. The phone at their flat had been disconnected because of an unpaid bill, so she wouldn't have been able to check up on him yet.

"Well, why not?" he said. "A nice hot whatsitsname – great!" He stood aside to let her bustle past him into the sitting room, then gingerly looked in after her. The cats had all returned. Indeed they seemed to have brought assorted cousins. They looked at him from chairs, from corners and from the back of the settee, with translucent eyes of green and gold.

"Oh, the dear little pussies," Sophie cried indulgently, as if they had all suddenly performed clever tricks. Jonny and the cats stared suspiciously at each other. "Now you sit down and I'll have something for you in just a moment." She made a courtly gesture suggesting the presence of white linen and table napkins and full settings of silver. Jonny edged into the room, afraid of causing another violent exodus.

"It's so nice to see you again," Sophie said. "Remember the good old days? Of course, I've been on my own for a year now. You never met Errol, did you? Such a dear, nice man, even though he wasn't a *professional* person, you know."

She chatted on, leaving nothing for Jonny to do except nod sympathetically now and then, and to remember someone else's good old days as well as he could. The cats turned out to be less horrified by a daytime-Jonny than they had been by the unknown man coming in out of the dark. Though several left the room in a pointed fashion, others leaped up from chairs and corners and began a nervous pacing – arching backs, rubbing themselves against furniture, tails erect, mewing in various voices. Last night's laid-back hero, the large black cat, yawned rudely and closed his eyes. He looked harder – *denser* – than the other cats, like a visitor from a cat planet with a much higher gravity than earth.

"I've got the milk bottle!" Sophie declared triumphantly, holding it aloft like the torch of liberty. "Those people next door had taken it, but I got it back." She chuckled, diving into the kitchen, taking the milk with her. "There are some funny people around these days," she confided, half whispering. She turned as Jonny came into the doorway and stood watching her.

In the light of day, free from night's confusions, Jonny could see that the kitchen not only shared a doorway with the sitting room but had another at the opposite end, probably leading into Sophie's bedroom. A third door, tucked in between the sink and a set of cupboards, led out on to the balcony. The shells on the windowsill, turned to show their linings of pearl and opal, suggested all over again that the rise and fall of the sound on the other side of the window might be the sea, that stepping out on to the balcony he might breathe in the scents of salt and seaweed. He might look down and see far, far below, white serpents of foam winding in and out of one another, breaking up, then joining together again.

"Might is right," Bonny joked in his head. "Might is write. It's all a story in a book." She had always been a reader.

Jonny reminded himself that what he could hear was merely the flow of traffic – the city breathing, panting rather heavily at this hour in the morning. He watched Sophie, wondering what to do next. With a bit of luck he could have been off down the road by now. Obviously, she remembered nothing of last night, and had had to reinvent him. Even now, busy with kitchen activities, what she was remembering was not the actual activities themselves, but the way it felt to be doing them.

She had all the gestures of a busy person, but nothing was happening. She shifted things from place to place, picking them up briskly, putting them down with an air of efficiency, even though she had done nothing with them.

"Listen, Sophie," Jonny said at last, "how about letting me fix something for you? You sit down on that stool and tell me about the old days, and I'll get us something to eat." He did not want to eat anything himself for he still felt queasy, and the kitchen surfaces were disagreeable, but Sophie looked pinched and frail, as if she would be the better for a good breakfast.

"Well, that *is* kind of you," she said, rather to his surprise, and sat down and talked happily about an old house, and mushrooming, and the school picnics they had apparently shared down by a river somewhere. "And remember the day that bull got into the school yard?" she cried, looking up at him dramatically.

Meanwhile, getting her something to eat was proving unexpectedly difficult. Jonny opened cupboards, making a series of remarkable discoveries – a set of false teeth smiling anxiously from a tumbler of clouded water, ancient, yellowing papers held together by a rubber band and slipped in a glove for further safety, an old telephone directory, a pink receipt for seven dollars signed *Spike*, dried orange peel and eggshells carefully saved in a screw-top jar – but no bread, no butter, no tea, no coffee. The knife drawer was tightly packed with many more packets of biscuits, all opened. One or two of them were edged with blue mould.

"You're certainly keen on biscuits, aren't you!" Jonny said, slowly smiling, and Sophie smiled back.

"I like to have something in the house," she confided, "because you never know who's going to pop in from nowhere."

"No," agreed Jonny. "You ought to be more careful. Not everyone's as nice as I am, you know."

"I don't like to be caught without any eatables," Sophie added, ignoring this.

"But you need more than biscuits for breakfast," Jonny pointed out. "You need porridge – or stewed apple or something. Tea! You can't start the day without a cuppa," he added, quoting his mother, and promptly imagined her at home finishing her cup of tea, and beginning to work on the robin costumes his little sisters would need for their elementary dance recital in the annual competitions – still a month away.

"A cup of tea! I'll get it right away," Sophie cried, leaping to her feet, just as if he had introduced a new and welcome possibility. She began to search the cupboards he had just searched himself, hopefully patting the barren shelves around the false teeth.

Inspired, Jonny opened the fridge but shut it abruptly. It held nothing but bottles of milk – about ten of them – and a dead blackbird in a pie-dish. The ancient patterning common to kitchens and middens had finally broken down in Sophie's house. It was the sort of place you might arrive at when everything else broke down – a place at the end of everything else.

"Anything goes!" Jonny sang softly under his breath, and his feet absent-mindedly repeated the rhythm of the phrase on the dirty lino. "Everything goes," Bonny told him out of memory. Sophie searched on hopefully. She was wearing an old petticoat, torn lace looping down from the hem, a jersey knitted from some light, synthetic yarn, another petticoat and, strangest of all (something Jonny had been trying not to notice), a white suspender-belt, its fastenings bobbing as she moved. Early as it was, her bowl-shaped hat was on her head, and thick stockings and woolly slippers covered her legs and feet. After a while her busy ferreting got on Jonny's nerves.

"There's nothing here but biscuits," he said impatiently.

"Yeees!" she said very slowly, looking into the air in a puzzled way, as if missing provisions might suddenly fall out from above, "and it's very funny because I had everything yesterday. I'm never without." Her whole face seemed to narrow, her mouth thinned with suspicion. "You know, sometimes I wonder about those people next door, because there's no doubt... things just vanish away. Those people could get a key to this place, you know and – and just come in and..." She flung out her hands in a dramatic gesture suggesting rape and pillage.

"Well," said Jonny, as lightly as he could, "I'll have to be off." He wondered about shaking hands, but found he was unwilling to touch her, partly because she seemed so brittle she might crumble away, but mostly because she was so dirty, and dirt on an old woman seemed particularly repellent. "Look, thanks for everything!" he said awkwardly. "You really saved my life last night." Her face brightened with pleasure and surprise.

"Did I?" she cried. "Well, I think it's a poor state of affairs if we can't help one another." She smiled warmly. "Particularly someone of your own," she added.

"Yes, well, thanks anyway, er – Sophie," Jonny said, turning to go, then turning back again. "Look, do get yourself some decent tucker, won't you?" he said rather irritably, alarmed to find himself worrying about her.

He saw the beginning of a wistful expression forming on her face, quickly waved at her, smiled, nodded reassuringly, turned once more and hurried off, putting the headphones of the Walkman on his head and over his ears so that he wouldn't hear her if she called after him.

"SHUT YOUR EARS BUT THE VOICE GOES WANDERING ON," jeered the band. His feet thudded slowly on the stairs. He opened the door. Outside, cars flowed along the one-way street, thin sunshine washed up over the footpath. For a moment it was all there before him, the way home – but Jonny hesitated in the doorway, staring right, staring left.

"TURNING ON THE WHEEL – TURNING ON THE WHEEL IN THE AIR," sang the band.

"Oh, hell," said Jonny with exasperation. He had just found he couldn't walk away and leave Sophie with nothing to eat except mouldy biscuits. Whether he liked it or not, something fair, even kind, in him made it difficult to walk off and leave her lost in her own kitchen. Jonny leaned in the doorway, scornful of his conscience, but unable to escape it.

"It'll only take me a little bit longer," he said to the door frame, making an excuse as if it had derided him. Turning like a wheel, he faced into Sophie's house once more, and began to climb the stairs again, his feet sounding heavier than they had as he was coming down.

CHAPTER FIVE

Sophie was almost as he had left her, still searching the shelves, frowning and muttering to herself.

"Oh dear, oh dear!" she was saying. "Oh dear, oh dear, oh dear."

"Hey!" Jonny said right behind her and she jumped convulsively, then turned and faced him defiantly. Her frightened expression changed at once.

"Oh, it's *you*!" she cried. "Come in. Do come in. Sit down! I'll have a cup of tea for you in next to no time. I remember just how you like it."

"Look – have you got any money on you?" Jonny asked her, coming right to the point. "Because if you have, I'll take you shopping and get you stocked up – fruit, eggs, bread made with stoneground flour – everything you ought to have."

Sophie gave him a glance so sweet and clear that he smiled back in involuntary wonder.

"That's very good of you, dear," she said, "but I can manage." She opened the knife drawer, rediscovering the biscuits. "Here we are!" she cried in delight. "I knew they were here somewhere."

A little later, having watched her sustain herself on gingernuts, stale sultana squares and hot water, Jonny again suggested that they go shopping. Sophie was pleased at the thought of the shops.

"I'll just get my walking shoes!" she said.

"While you're there how about taking those... extra clothes off?" Jonny said, not being too specific about just what she should remove. "Put on a dress." He glanced furtively at the suspender-belt.

Sophie gave him a look of gentle reproach.

"I don't tell *you* what to wear," she said in a soft but determined voice, vanishing into her bedroom. When she came out again she was carrying her handbag and wearing a coat which, having several buttons, concealed the strange ensemble beneath. But her walking shoes were terribly down at heel and misshapen. Jonny led the way out of the house, just in case he had to catch her, for it was easy to imagine those shoes treacherously pitching her forward down the stairs. He slapped his pockets as he went, checking on his wallet and his post-office savings book.

"Those people next door," Sophie said, looking resentfully over at the neighbouring doorstep. "They're always taking my milk, you know, but I don't argue with them. I just slip over and take it back. And look at the state of their letterbox. Errol sold the houses, I think, otherwise

they'd never be allowed to have a letterbox like that."
Jonny agreed that he had seen better letterboxes. "I think
the landlord might live there now," Sophie's elegant voice
flowed on with barely a pause. "You know, when Errol was
alive, I never bothered with rent, but now I have to pay it
all the time. I always get a receipt, of course."

Their shopping began at the post office where Jonny
withdrew some money himself. He still had a little bit in
this old account, though most of his money, earned during
the days when he and Janine had been the Chickenbits
stars, was invested in a finance company his father had
chosen. It had never really seemed like his (not even as
much as the dole payments did) though, from time to
time, he was allowed to spend some of it. His recent fine
for disorderly behaviour had been paid out of dancing
money; he would soon have to pay another.

Beside him, Sophie muttered over the form, becoming
more and more agitated. She pushed the point of the post-
office pen hard down on the paper, apparently hoping to
squeeze written words out of it by force but she had
forgotten how to begin moving it along. In the end Jonny
guided her, reading her account number aloud to her, telling
her where to write her name, and spelling it aloud for her.

"The girl at the desk sometimes helps me," she
confided in him. "They're very good to me here."

"I'm glad you've got some savings," Jonny said in a
startled voice, noticing the respectable total in Sophie's

post-office savings account. He had judged from her house, hat and handbag that she must be very poor.

"Errol was a good saver," Sophie replied as they went down the steps. "Of course, that class of people had to be. It made me realise how extravagant *we* used to be in the good old days. Errol had a very hard time when he was a boy, you know. And then he went through the First World War."

"Well, we're both rich now, Sophie," Jonny replied. "Let's spend it." They crossed the road rather erratically, tooted at by a white van, which actually seemed to swerve towards them, roaring from a faulty exhaust. Sophie stopped in the middle of the street, prepared to argue with it, but Jonny pulled her after him and only looked after the van when they were safe on the opposite footpath. They walked past The Colville pub and came to some shops.

"Here are the cakes!" Sophie cried joyously, and led him with great confidence into a sort of milkbar, where the proprietor was setting out trays of sandwiches, and cakes shrouded in cheesecloth.

To one side of the shop was a table covered with a gingham table-cloth and flanked by two chairs.

The shop assistant hovered protectively behind the counter while Sophie chose her cakes, for she refused to use the tongs and tried to put certain unsatisfactory cakes back after she had inspected them closely.

Jonny was surprised to find himself embarrassed by such behaviour. He had thought he was beyond such things. As it was, he stood uneasily at Sophie's elbow, sighing and shaking his head to show the assistant that he was not at all sympathetic with such poor conduct.

"Sophie! You've touched it! You've *breathed* on it," he cried in the very accents of his mother.

"But this one's nice," Sophie said, squeezing her second cake until it seemed it must squeak in protest.

"Live it up! Have both," Jonny suggested, and the shop assistant smiled.

Sophie roared with laughter. "Have both!" she repeated. "Oh dear, oh dear! Have both!"

But she did take both, and paid for tea and cakes in the manner of a little girl seriously spending pocket-money for the first time. When she got the change she stood holding it, looking at it very hard, rather as Jonny had looked at the name of Marribel Road inscribed in his palm.

"Taking her in hand, are you? " said the shop assistant, obviously curious about such an unlikely escort for a notorious customer. "Time somebody did!"

They sat on either side of the plate of cakes and Sophie poured proper-coloured tea.

Well, thought Jonny, I suppose there are worse places.

"It's a cloudless sky! Quite cloudless!" Sophie announced, staring raptly up into the air. Jonny looked up, too. The ceiling was painted plain blue. Under Sophie's gaze it took on depth and height. Refusing to let his eyes be stopped by the plain surface Jonny stared intently into it just as she was doing. It quietly grew deep – deeper – until it went on for ever. While he gazed upward, astonished at the power of her suggestion, she took another cake, holding it in her knobbly hand, opening her mouth and sticking her tongue out slightly as the cake approached it. Turning away from the infinite milkbar ceiling, thinking she resembled some old parrot eating seeds, but dressed up in a coat and hat, he noticed in a vaguely troubled way that the front of her coat was very badly stained.

Who exactly *was* Sophie? Someone with a whole history but a broken memory. She had been married, so she might even have children somewhere. One thing he was certain of: in the past, when she had had a more normal understanding, she would never have appeared in public in clothes stained with food. She would never have dressed with a suspender-belt on top.

Jonny took a cake of his own, but he didn't eat it, just sat holding it, looking up at the blue ceiling again, remembering other expanses of sky and sea. It was strange that something could be so beautiful at the same time as it was so nightmarish.

"Was it my fault?" Jonny had cried. "I was right behind her."

"Don't tell them!" Bonny had said. "I'll say you were up here with me." She had crossed her arms over her breast and

was hugging herself to stop her trembling, but in spite of that the bracelets on her wrists and the gold and silver chains around her throat gave off a faint, continual chime. The rings on her fingers, the stars painted in silver on the full sleeves of her black chiffon blouse, had glittered in the evening light because of her trembling. "I'll say you were up here with me," she repeated. "They won't ask you any questions." Then she stopped hugging herself, and hugged Jonny instead. They stood embracing behind the danger sign. But that was all a long time ago.

Sophie coughed politely. Across the table she was unfolding her paper napkin. She stared down at it very hard for a moment, then looked up and smiled at Jonny. "I like a good book," she said, "but the print's too small in this one." Jonny sat with the uneaten cake in his hand, and saw her looking at it rather wistfully. He put it on her plate.

"Always the gentleman!" she said, with a gracious inclination of her head. Then she ate the cake, leaving a small moustache of cream. A little later they left the shop, side by side. Catching sight of their reflections, distorted by the glass, Jonny thought they looked ill-assorted, but matching, too. They were both derelicts.

In the grocer's, Sophie made purposefully for the racks of biscuits but Jonny successfully distracted her with tea, instant coffee, eggs, butter, a loaf of sliced wholemeal bread and a tin of sardines. He also suggested she buy a large box of dried cat food. He bought himself a toothbrush as if he intended to stay another night in Sophie's house, when really he was determined to go home as soon as he had got her back to her own kitchen and had given her something to eat. In the fruit shop he spent his own money on oranges, tomatoes and a lettuce. The thought of leaving her well-supplied eased the feeling that he was leaving someone who needed help, adrift on the indifferent tides of the city.

"It's not as if I owe her anything – well, not much," he whispered, nodding as he agreed with himself. Nobody would blame him if he went home after this. It would be a normal decision. Yet he was also fascinated at finding himself there, one disintegrating star in orbit around another.

Opposite the fruit shop was an electrician's business: *F. J. Fowler* – a relation of terrible Nev's, no doubt. Nev had been born in Colville, lived all his life in Colville, had many Colville relatives. Just having the name *Fowler* had made him feel justified in dominating others. Colville was saturated with Nev. At any moment he might come around the corner on his bike, his knife at his side, and then...

"Damn Nev!" Jonny said softly. "I don't have to be scared of him any more."

They wandered back along the street. Autumn sunshine was still rich and warm. The wind had a little edge to it, suggesting invisible mountains and garden fires, crisp, dried leaves rustling down under the chestnut trees by the river, and somewhere, far to the west, snow on the mountains. Jonny looked narrowly at the city. It seemed reasonable enough today, with nothing to suggest the displacements of last night. Yet every now and then he felt he was moving through one of Bonny's old stories which had been about disguises, bewildering encounters, magical changes. If Janine had sometimes seemed to give off light, Bonny had taken it in, so that he always remembered her as shadowy. Her stories and grave jokes gave off the light by which he saw her most clearly.

"Ah, here are the cakes!" cried Sophie, in the triumphant voice of someone making a welcome discovery, as they returned past the dairy.

"We've had cakes already," Jonny pointed out sternly, steering her on, refusing to meet the eye of the assistant who peered out at them apprehensively.

"*I* haven't had any," Sophie cried crossly, and was inclined to sulk, until she saw a new goal directly ahead.

"I'll just go into the post office and get some money out!" she cried. "It doesn't do to run yourself short."

"Been there, done that," said Jonny impatiently. In the end, he had to take her post-office savings book from her bag, searching through clogged combs, milk-bottle tops, and several uneaten biscuits folded in an old Christmas card in order to find it. When he shook the money accusingly under her nose, she looked surprised, but then beamed radiantly at him.

"I'm glad you told me about that," she said in a cosy voice, smiling approvingly. "You've saved me a lot of trouble."

"You took it out yourself," Jonny said.

"I think men understand money better than women do," Sophie confided.

"You sweet, old-fashioned girl!" Jonny replied snappily.

Sophie looked very pleased at being called sweet and old-fashioned. "I don't always think things have changed for the best," she confided complacently. They stopped at the traffic lights before the railway line. A train was going by very, very slowly. Carriages glided evenly in front of them, while on their right, cars growled and muttered. The lights changed. The cars leaped forward like trained cheetahs and rushed, released, down the one-way street.

Ahead of them the two houses stood side by side like prim sisters. In the light of day the giant tap was a primitive blue, the balcony thrust out beneath it like an aggressive lip. But who would ever want to sit on that balcony with the tap poised above, ready to drown the city? Who would want a nice view, across the flow of the one-way street, to the business opposite? *Industrial Gloves Ltd*, Jonny read.

Someone seemed to be watching them from the balcony of the house next door, but in the daylight Jonny could see that last night's alien was only an old dummy from a dress shop, its extended hands turned up as if it were checking, right and left, for rain. It had no face, no hair – only a rather elegant oval head tilted on its long neck to stare down at them. "Hi, there!" Jonny said, raising his hand to it. It still looked alien, naked but sexless, eyeless but aware of them.

Meanwhile, Sophie was scrummaging madly in her bag, mumbling to herself.

"Try the string around your neck," Jonny suggested.

"Well," she cried in amazement a moment later. "I'm glad you drew my attention to that. You've saved me a lot of trouble." She opened her door.

"113," Jonny said, reading her number from the letterbox. "Do you think that's a lucky number, Sophie?"

"I think it must be," she replied. "I am lucky, you know. Not that I bet on horses, but I find a lot of money in the street. People often drop, say, sixpence and don't notice it."

"It isn't called sixpence any more," Jonny said. "It's called five cents these days."

"I'm glad you put me right about that," said Sophie, leading the way back into her house. "I don't think they should interfere with money, do you? Of course, in the past, Errol managed all my money for me, but now I have to do it for myself, and I've got to be careful, because my memory isn't as good as it was."

Cats spoke enquiringly out of the gloom at the top of the stair.

"Oh, the pussies!" Sophie said. "They're glad to see us back."

"Puss, puss!" Jonny said, placating the natives.

CHAPTER SIX

Now, thought Jonny, dropping the bagful of oranges on a chair. No more mucking around! She's got food in the house. It's time to go.

"I'll have a cup of tea for us in next to no time," Sophie promised in the cosy voice of a woman indulging a helpless male.

"No. Forget it. I'll be off in a minute," Jonny said, absent-mindedly pulling the curtains back from the sitting-room windows which looked on to the backyard.

Autumn sunshine edged into the room which began to sparkle with numberless particles of dust. Directly in front of him was a backyard fenced in with corrugated iron which had once been painted green. Among the weeds, lengths of spouting rusted quietly; he could make out earthenware and metal pipes, even an old hand-basin slumped among the green leaves and black berries of nightshade, and long blades of rank grasses – all growing between cracked expanses of concrete. To the right was a sort of fossil of plumbing – a tank mounted high on a spindly tank stand, though water pressure must have come to this part of the city a long time ago. Underneath everything else he could make out a faint pattern – the ghost of an old order. There had once been a garden here, and a past arrangement of old beds and borders still haunted the backyard though, when he tried to look at it directly, this ghost-garden lost itself in its own weeds. Cats, curled in all the crevices, leaped to their feet as Jonny opened the windows to flood the room with comparatively fresh air. Beyond the tanks was a wall, beyond that again another neglected garden and an even taller wall, the same one Jonny had seen the night before when he had drawn the curtains. It was quite shadowless in the daytime.

Turning, he detected a quizzical expression on Sophie's face. She was not altogether pleased with the open window but did not say anything immediately.

"Fresh air!" Jonny said, setting a good example by breathing deeply. "It's good for you, Soph!"

"Oh, yes, I suppose so," she replied pettishly. Jonny pushed a chair towards her with his foot, and she sat on it obediently, while he pulled another chair to face the first one. He wanted her to listen very carefully to what he was about to say, so, sitting himself down and facing her he made himself take her hands. Her fingernails, as long as witch's nails, grazed his palms, and this thin trace laid against his skin made him prickle all over.

What's wrong with me? thought Jonny impatiently.

She's just old and a bit… His thoughts ran out. He was nineteen, liked to think he had learned to be tough, able to give and take blows, yet he could scarcely bear to touch Sophie. All the same, she had really caught his attention. Collapsing little by little in her collapsing house she still battled on with everything she had. Besides, she perceived the world oddly. If she wasn't a Pythoness, she was some other sort of oracle. *Are you the one?* she had asked him significantly. If Jonny had had the sense to reply confidently, she might have burst into rhyme as Bonny had once done.

Bonny, too, had dressed remarkably in clothes she decorated herself by painting pictures on them, by adding ribbons or Christmas decorations, or stars of silver paper. She had a box of rings and chains of tinsel, bottletops and bracelets that tinkled. Dressed in all this glory, she would slide the snake ring on to the third finger of her left hand (marrying magic, she called it) and would tell the future or give wise advice in rhyme.

But as they ran out of the reserve to get help (knowing already that no help could arrive in time) Jonny had seen her pull the serpent ring from her finger and throw it away. The meadowy grasses were golden in the evening light, and the ring flew over them like a golden insect – not a butterfly, something smaller and more compact… a bee, or a rare ant-queen in her wedding dress.

And so here he was, sitting in Sophie's house, feeling those long fingernails scrape against his palm.

"Sophie!" he said very loudly and clearly as if he were speaking to someone deaf. "Listen to me." The blankness of her stare demolished him. There was no one at home behind those sweet, faded blue eyes, no one at all. "Are you listening to me, Sophie?" he said, trying again, shaking her hands slightly to compel all the attention she had to give.

"Of course I am," she replied briskly, returning his grasp, though her gaze was still vacant. The things she saw best were all locked in behind her wide, square forehead. It was only because he had matched up with something in that inside world that she was noticing him at all.

"Sophie! Have you got any family? Any children? Does anyone, you know, keep an eye on you?" He could imagine his mother's feelings if she found, on one of her regular visits to his own granny, that a strange, battered young man had moved in. Sophie stared back at him. Her eyes, with almost no eyebrows and barely any lashes, were touchingly naked. There was nothing to be read in them. When she frowned it was more in an effort to please him than because she was really trying to work anything out.

"Any children?" she repeated very slowly, like somebody deciphering a language she barely knew. "No. No, I don't think so."

"Or any family or friends?" he persisted. "Now that

Errol's dead... Have you got any nephews or nieces who pop in to see you?"

Her eyes brightened. She had made a sure connection.

"I always have a few biscuits on hand, you know," she told him. "You have to have something in the house, in case someone just pops in from nowhere."

Jonny sighed. Keeping a few biscuits in the house was beginning to feel like one of the great eternal ideas people talked about, ideas like Truth and Justice. However, he felt certain no family or friends had visited Sophie for a long, long time. Her disorder had the mark of a long, slow, solitary evolution, without any outside interference. Quite unaware of evolving in any direction, Sophie leaned back in her chair and sighed.

"I feel a bit tired," she confided. "It's a long walk down to that place, you know, that *thingummy* where you get the whatsitsnames."

But then she leaped abruptly from her chair and slammed the windows shut, banging each frame firmly with the heel of her hand to make sure it was firmly latched, before sitting down again. Jonny picked up their purchases and carried them into the kitchen.

"I'll make one in a minute," she called drowsily after him. Jonny dumped the bags beside the sink, listening all the time to the stop-and-go voice of the one-way street. He rattled the door that led on to the balcony, but it was locked. On a hook beside the door were several keys, lightly veiled in cobwebs. The one on the top, a key for a Yale lock, was probably for the front door. Jonny took it off the hook, put it on the kitchen counter and took the next one which looked quite promising. It fitted grudgingly, but he had to turn it using the handle of a teaspoon as a lever. At last the door groaned and opened, and Jonny went out on to the balcony, nearly decapitating himself with a clothes line that stretched diagonally across it. He unhooked the loop of rope nearest the door, nodding to the dummy on the balcony of the house next door.

Below him, the road darted with schools of cars. Overhead the tap curved down at him, like the beak of a predator. One peck, and he would vanish for ever. From here he could see it was quite solid. No water would ever rush out of it to drown the city. On his left, the shop dummy gazed blindly across the street, arms outspread in the gesture of a clever conjuror drawing an audience's attention to an amazing revelation, or perhaps of someone yearning for industrial gloves; to the right, the city spread itself generously before him. Not far away he could see the irregular green dip that marked the curve of the river, its banks planted with willows and poplars. Further west he could make out the pillowy outline of the English trees in the city park and beyond them, but miles and miles away, the spiky peaks of the mountains. The world was still in place.

Reassured, Jonny went back to the kitchen, and began unpacking. Air flowing in from the street below was full of dust and petrol fumes, but he felt Sophie's house would be better for any change. He pulled the headphones of the Walkman up over his head, settled them firmly against his ears, and turned on the cassette.

"DREAM CITY, DREAM STREET..." sang the band. "ALWAYS AT MY DOOR."

Whistling, Jonny found a bowl for the oranges and left them where Sophie would be certain to see them. However, when he opened the fridge to put the butter and the eggs away he encountered the blackbird once more. While he stood staring at it dubiously, cats, excited by the opening of the fridge, came running in. Some stopped short on seeing who was in the kitchen, but others clustered around him. Within seconds he was surrounded by them.

"Take it! It's all yours!" Jonny said, gingerly tipping the bird on to the floor. The cats sniffed at it eagerly, but immediately looked into the fridge, sure that even better things would be brought out for them. In the end Jonny opened the dried cat food and sprinkled pellets on the floor, ignoring the saucers of sour milk and sliced banana.

"I'll get rid of the worst of this mess," he told them. But once he started he went on under a kitchen-spell, for tidying up turned out to be hypnotic. It was reassuring to be bringing some sort of order out of chaos, even in a small way, classifying and collating (spoons in one place, knives in another, biscuits in a proper tin) and wiping down dirty surfaces.

One of his first and most welcome discoveries was of a supply of blue plastic bin-liners, and one of the first things to go out was the unfortunate blackbird. "Sing a song of sixpence," sang Jonny to the cats, wondering if Sophie had been planning to save it until she had twenty-four of them. He went on tidying up, fascinated by the surface of a life even more incoherent than his own. A cake of soap sat cosily in the sugar bowl where it fitted very well; a series of tiny newspaper parcels carefully sealed with Sellotape proved to hold one used tea bag apiece. Jonny studied these things with the absorption of a hunter following a trail.

For a while he stood reading a notebook with an orange cover, full of names, addresses, phone numbers and little lists. Once upon a time, probably in the beginning, when her memory was just beginning to let her down, Sophie had fought back by making many lists... of birthdays, of dates when income-tax payments would fall due, a series of dates under the general heading *Rent* which seemed to be paid once a month. There was even a list of the numbers of lottery tickets Sophie had bought, and a few pages over, another of coins found in the street.

From under a pile of paper bags, all neatly straightened and folded, Jonny drew a small cream-coloured transistor radio, its dials and knobs picked out in gold. He turned it on idly. To his astonishment a gravelly male voice, distorted but still understandable, spoke out of it, and gave him the time and news headlines. He turned off his Walkman and listened keenly. Motorbike gangs had clashed at a football practice somewhere in the North Island, and one man was suffering from knife wounds. Road deaths were slightly up on the same time last year, whereas overseas butter sales were down. Striking workers at a petrol refinery had agreed to go back to work, and Hinerangi Hotene, the beautiful young activist who had thrown an explosive at the Minister for Maori Affairs was still on the run. Mountain rescue teams were looking for two missing climbers, and there was concern for their safety as they were thought to be lightly-clad for the prevailing conditions. Jonny was surprised to hear such up-to-the-minute news coming from an old, frail, plastic toy like Sophie's radio.

Putting it on top of the refrigerator, he opened the cupboard under the sink. What he found there was so dismaying that he took off his blazer and hung it on a hook on the wall before gingerly removing a small orange bucket filled with something pale and festering which he put over by the cats' saucers, together with three disgusting tea-towels. He would deal with them later. Pulling the stained newspaper from the shelves before replacing it with something new and clean, Jonny found himself staring at what seemed to be a lining of five-dollar notes. A closer glance showed him they were fifties. There was about six hundred dollars, some of it damp and rotting, stuck to the wooden slats under Sophie's sink.

It was almost embarrassing... so much naked money in such abandoned circumstances.

Take me! it said, lying back voluptuously in front of him. Even in decay it was attractive. *You deserve me,* it said suggestively. Jonny counted it twice before sliding it back reluctantly under fresh paper. Just handling it made him feel rich and secure, particularly when he was certain Sophie had forgotten it was there. She wouldn't miss it, he thought. I could leave a receipt, and suddenly he saw one of his own eyes looking back at him out of a little handbag mirror, propped at the back of a shelf. He shifted his head, assessing his face patched with storm-cloud colours. Very shifty, he thought, turning away, and turning on his Walkman too, so that loud music might drive all temptation from him.

Perhaps it was these very temptations that made him notice with sudden suspicion the pile of pink receipts in the knife drawer under a packet of gingernuts. They were all for small amounts of money – five dollars, nine dollars, three dollars – and were all signed *Spike*. He had noticed others like them lying around the house. The handwriting was clear and rather childish, and they all seemed reasonably new, with none of the faded, grubby look acquired by other old bills and receipts. Spike, thought Jonny. I'll bet!

"IT'S A STRIP OFF! IT'S A RIP OFF!" sang the band. ("Smile!" called Jonny's mother, as she often did at inappropriate moments. "Step, shuffle, ball-change – and smile.")

Jonny automatically danced and smiled and looked happy, though more like a Wolfman in disguise than a tap-dancer. It takes one to know one, he thought, holding one of the receipts up to the light. All in all, as housework went, there was a lot of variety in Sophie's kitchen. All this time Sophie slept in the sitting room, slumped in a chair, her head bent forward so that he could see the pinkness of her head under her thin, white, unwashed hair. An exploitative cat had settled itself in her lap and two young cats, little more than kittens, raced backwards and forwards in front of her, playing at ambushes and dangerous encounters.

"WHEN THE WORLD EXPLODES WE'LL BE DANCING IN THE DUST," sang the band.

Jonny looked around the kitchen and decided it was tidy enough. The surfaces, the sink, the cupboard doors were wiped down, cups hung on cup-hooks, plates were piled neatly according to size, saucepans nested cosily inside one another. String, rubberbands, bills, receipts and the orange notebook were all together in one drawer. The cats' saucers were washed. The floor was still dirty and the fridge needed defrosting, but enough was enough.

"I've certainly earned my way," Jonny said aloud, and glanced at the cupboard where the money was hidden. All that was left to do was to find a place to put the dirty tea-towels, always supposing it was worth trying to salvage them.

"DOWN DOWN DOWN DOWN! DOWN IS THE WAY TO THE BIG MACHINE," sang the band. Jonny nodded. Of course, Errol, master plumber and one of nature's gentlemen, would not have wished his wife to do the washing in the bath. Picking up the orange bucket and the dirty tea-towels, he ran lightly downstairs, pushed past the supermarket trolley full of shoes and found, beyond the stairs, a small, desperate, grey room opening out into the ghost-garden, and containing not only a washing machine and tubs, but an ironing board, tilted slightly sideways, like a crippled grasshopper. Jonny's eyes widened; his lips compressed. The ironing board was covered with a blanket and a sheet, and all over the surface of the sheet, sometimes going right through the blanket to the metal beneath, were black triangular tracks. Electricity, given more freedom than it should have had, had left a dangerous trail in Sophie's laundry. The iron itself stood precariously at the very end of the ironing board in the place provided. It was still plugged in and switched on, but it was covered with a sort of burnt toffee that suggested it was quite cold. The cord was frayed, and where it entered its plug, Jonny glimpsed the bright tinsel of fine wire.

"Oh, God!" he said. "The silly old bat."

As he said this, he heard slow steps on the stairs. Sophie was awake. Jonny did not go to meet her immediately, but remained trying to work out if there might be anything here which was likely to explode in a fountain of blue sparks, setting the house on fire. The door opened and closed, and then he heard the key turn in the lock. He was locked in with the cats, staring at a wall full of laundry shelves – neat but very dusty, filled with more packets of yellow washing soap than Sophie could hope to use up in the rest of her life: packets of detergent, floor polish, oven cleaner and disinfectant. A carpet-sweeper stood to attention at the end of the shelves. The sight of so many substances intended to keep a house clean in a house so abandoned to dirt and decay filled Jonny with a familiar uneasiness.

When she comes back, I'll slip out and go home, he thought. I'll just get my blazer... He heard the door rattle slightly. Sophie was already trying to get back in.

Jonny pushed past the trolley of shoes and shouted to her. "Sophie, can you hear me?"

"Ye-es," she replied, making two querulous words of it. "I'm locked out. Someone has taken my key, and I've got to stand here holding this big, heavy whatsitsname."

"Try the string around your neck," Jonny shouted back.

"The string around my neck?" repeated Sophie. "I don't

tie string around my neck." But all the same she must have found it, because as Jonny was drawing a breath to explain still further she spoke again in a relieved voice.

"I always keep my keys there, because if you lose them, well, anyone could find them and just come walking into the house." Jonny heard the key scratching in the lock. The door opened, and there was Sophie holding the key in one hand and a very heavy book in the other. She stared at him doubtfully.

"Remember me?" said Jonny. "Remember the good old days?" But Sophie looked as if she might not remember them. "I've been tidying the house for you."

"I suppose that's all right," Sophie said, still doubtful. She held out the book towards him. "Just tell me, what do you make of this?"

"It's a book," Jonny said, taking it and reading the title. *A History of Angels.*

"Why did he give it to me?" Sophie asked.

"Who?" asked Jonny, though now he came to think of it, it was strange that she should go outside and return within a minute carrying such a thing.

"What do you make of it?" she repeated.

"I didn't know there were so many," Jonny replied, looking at *A History of Angels* with respect. "I thought there was just Matthew, Mark, Luke and whatshisname."

"They breed, you know," she said significantly, "and then they take over from the nice people."

Jonny opened the front cover.

"Bonny Benedicta," he read aloud. He thought he must be having an intense, momentary dream, but the words would not go away. Jonny hit his head with his free hand, hoping to bump loose circuits back into place, but neither the name nor the book changed.

"Did you say some man gave this to you?" he asked.

"He was wearing pink – thingummy – yellow! What do you make of it?" repeated Sophie looking quite bewildered. Jonny put the book down.

"Excuse me," he told her. "I'll check it out." Then he leaped past her, almost tumbling out into Marribel Road. The door closed sharply behind him.

CHAPTER SEVEN

Out in the road, Jonny looked desperately up and down hoping to see someone, anyone, who might have given Sophie the book with Bonny's name in it. Yet he hardly expected he would. It had appeared like a vision, only available to him because he was standing close to Sophie who was a sort of magical fool. Cars streamed by so continuously that it seemed impossible that anyone could have crossed the road and vanished into *Industrial Gloves,* for example, but on his own side of the road the only person in sight was far, far away and rapidly retreating. Jonny gave chase, but long before he was near enough to call to him, the man got into a car and drove away. Jonny, still holding the book, slowed down, but did not turn back. Instead he went on wandering down Marribel Road reading doors and signs, for if Sophie could go out into the street for a few minutes and then return with Bonny's name in a book about angels, then the tide of accident was certainly flowing his way at last. "What do you make of it?" Sophie had asked. It would be mad to ignore such a clue.

At first his expectations were unreasonably exalted. All might be magically revealed – he might come on a sign saying *Pythoness Services Ltd,* or the emblem of the wise serpent twisted into a ring. Marribel Road did have plenty to say – *Oppose Homosexual Law Reform* or *Save the Whales.* But it was shouting to the world, not whispering to Jonny.

There were no houses in Marribel Road, at least no houses where people lived family lives. Of course, Bonny might work here somewhere. University students often had part-time jobs if they could get them. Slowly, as he accepted that there would be no instant revelation, Jonny's walk became aimless. Going to the top of Marribel Road he paused by yet another set of traffic lights, then walked all the way back down the other side, passing Sophie's house with barely a glance. By then the constant, nervous roar of the traffic had begun to annoy him, and he turned impulsively down a thin alley called Ribbon Lane, coming out of it on to the river bank. Suddenly, Jonny knew exactly where he was... not far from Colville School, not very far from the house his family had lived in during the years they had been Colville people.

A pretty, melancholy stretch of winding road followed the river. On his left, willows and poplars, still wearing most of their autumn leaves, leaned towards the water. This sad autumnal beauty touched the old well-cared-for houses that looked across the river to the opposite bank, where more willows intermittently masked a curving road, a twin to the one he was walking along but lively with cars and commerce. As these cars sped by, ripples of colour, skipping like bright arrows across the surface of the dark water, sped beside him. Lured on by a strange mixture of nostalgia and loathing, Jonny went very slowly along the stretch of grass between the poplars and the willows, struck by the knobbly look of the roots sticking grey elbows up out of the soil. He had been hunted more than once along this very strip of ground by bigger boys shouting, "Chick-chick-chick-chick-chicken!" and threatening to wring his neck when they caught him. Around *this* bend they had cut him off. Jonny stood still, staring darkly at the particular poplar against which he had been pinned by bodies and bicycles while his school bag was rifled, and they drew on his face with his own felt pens a bright red mouth with swollen lips and spiky black eyelashes. Then they had made him dance. Jonny's feet danced automatically at the memory of it, for they had a twitchy sub-memory of their own. Jonny cooperated, holding the book as a partner... step on the right foot, shuffle on the left, a-one, a-two, and three, pause, four. "Smile, Jonny," his mother commanded from the past. "You're supposed to be happy." He did a small succession of muffled grab-offs in and out of the poplar roots, but with no audience this time except a white van, which roared around the next bend and, catching him in the act, tooted derisively.

"That's entertainment," Jonny shouted after the van, knowing he was also shouting to the invisible past-Jonny who danced for ever on this river bank.

"They only want attention," his mother had said, helping him to wash away the swollen scarlet lips and the spiky eyelashes. She was sympathetic but didn't think it was worth making a fuss over.

"They don't dare touch him if I'm around," Janine had declared, and this was true. "Ring the school! Don't let them get away with it." For once she had been on Jonny's side, almost shining with fury in the ordinary front room of their Colville house. "It's that repulsive Nev Fowler! He likes me, and I can't stand him. He only picks on Jonny so that I'll notice him. Well, I'm not going to. I'm going to look right through him as if he wasn't there."

"You'll never be a man until you learn to fight your own battles," his father explained, sounding not so much scornful as hurt, rather as if Jonny had broken a serious promise. Jonny had never doubted that his father loved him, though it was a confused sort of love which forbade him to protect Jonny in case Jonny never learned to take care of himself. He seemed to understand the Colville boys better than he understood Jonny. "You see?" he cried to Jonny's mother. "He may be good at it, but it's going to get him into all sorts of trouble when he tries to mix with boys – ordinary boys. He plays with girls too much."

It was Jonny's dancing he was protesting about, though

the money impressed him more than he liked to admit. Here, at the scene of past terror and humiliation, Jonny danced a little longer, half hoping someone would appear and challenge him, giving him the chance to show Colville that he had become a force to be reckoned with. Giving in to rage, knowing that he was about to be lost in passion, always filled him with an odd relief. There were times when he anticipated this loss of self with pleasure. But as he danced there on the river bank he was haunted by an even older pleasure. For a moment everything seemed as if it might be about to fall back into place, click into a true pattern. Jonny stopped dancing, but nevertheless felt light-hearted because of having done it.

"I'm still the master," he boasted to his feet, his words lost in the roar of the white van's return. The driver might have been anxious to take another look at him, but Jonny did not spare it a glance. He crossed the road, walked up a street that he did not know but which looked as if it should lead somewhere, and so it did, for in due course it delivered him to the railway line, a thread that would lead him back to Marribel Road.

"Well, what now?" Jonny asked himself. Should he go home, make peace with his parents, and then, maybe, ring one of the Dr Benedictas at work explaining that he had come into possession of a book of Bonny's which he wanted to return to her. Or should he forget about seeing Bonny at all? Even if he found her, what on earth was he planning to say? Yet he could feel, running through his mind, as a thread might run between finger and thumb, a clue of chance that he was unwilling to abandon. At this moment the wind blew cold on him. He shivered, recalling that he had left his blazer on a hook in Sophie's kitchen. With open exasperation and a secret, irrational relief, he understood that he must return. Thrusting his hands into the pocket of his jeans as he came to this conclusion, he found, just as if it were waiting for this very moment, the Yale key to Sophie's front door.

Having walked back to Sophie's house, Jonny stood on the other side of the road studying it rather mistrustfully. The traffic lights changed to red, the cars stopped and built up in long columns back along Marribel Road. Jonny darted and danced between them, unlocked Sophie's door and went inside.

He had only been gone an hour and a half, but the house felt different, although he couldn't immediately say what the difference was. Of course, he had begun to change things himself. The smell at the bottom of the stairs was less thick with corruption. Opening windows had loosened the solid fug of years. Overhead, he could hear a great shuffling and banging. Drawers and cupboards were being opened and slammed shut. A perpetual and anxious search was in progress.

Several cats watched Jonny come up the stairs, mewing and arching their backs. One came several paces to meet him, a young white cat with tortoiseshell splotches and the trick, which some cats have, of mewing soundlessly. He could see her pink grimace and pointed teeth, but there was not even the squeak of a sound. Jonny put out his hand towards her, and she rose gracefully on her hind legs, so that she could have the top of her head stroked while still maintaining a discreet distance.

When he went into the sitting room he knew at once that, while he had been out wandering in Colville, Sophie had had a visitor. He could not only smell cigarettes, he actually saw a butt stubbed out on a saucer he had washed only a couple of hours earlier, and felt, for the first time in his life, the fury of a careful housekeeper outraged at the callousness of others.

Scuttling mouse-like around her sitting room, Sophie was carefully rearranging everything – tidying up, Jonny supposed she might have called it. Indeed, since he had left it, the room had undergone many small but significant changes. Cushions that had been on one chair were now on another, the pigeon-holes in the desk now held a dish-mop, a salt-cellar and a pair of glasses with one lens missing. The heater was full on, and cups and saucers were set out in front of it, rather as if Sophie were planning to picnic there. The two fairly clean tea-towels he had left in the kitchen were draped carefully over the back of the tartan settee. Even Sophie had changed. She was wearing a blue dress, though Jonny could see she had put it on over everything she had been wearing previously. When Jonny came bounding in, she looked at him with alarm.

"I've just paid!" she cried dramatically. "And now my handbag has vanished away."

"Just paid what?" asked Jonny, bristling with suspicion.

"I got a receipt," she cried defensively, looking over at the table.

"You don't have to pay anything," Jonny told her. "It's me."

"Who's me?" she asked rather tartly. Jonny saw his blazer hanging on a coat-hanger from the shelf over the empty fireplace and quickly retrieved it. It sounded as if Sophie might be about to order him to leave.

"Me!" he said cautiously. "You know who I am."

There on the edge of the table was a familiar pink receipt, unmistakably crisp and new and cleanly folded. Jonny picked it up and opened it. *"Spike,"* he read. Sophie was unreliable but he was certain that she had got things right for once. A landlord of some kind had just called in, she had paid rent and been given a receipt.

"How much rent do you pay?" he asked, looking at the figure mentioned. "Nine dollars? It's got to be more than that."

"Oh, it's *you*!" Sophie suddenly exclaimed. "I thought it was the landlord." She began to cast twinkling glances at him. "I'll get you a cup of tea at once. I remember just how you like it. No chance of my forgetting that."

Jonny waved the receipt at her.

"How much?" he insisted.

"I never get behind with it," Sophie said earnestly. "I pay as I go. Errol was very particular about things like that. 'If I pay cash, will you give me a discount?' he used to say. Dear old Errol. If ever there was one of nature's gentlemen, Errol was the man. Now I must make that cup of tea."

"Do you remember how I like it?" Jonny asked rather sourly, and she gave him a smile that suggested secrets between them. Following her into the kitchen, he checked the hoard under the sink. It was still there. He opened the newly tidied drawer to put the receipt away with the rest and saw that it had been rearranged during his absence. The orange notebook, the neatly coiled lengths of string and the rubber bands were all gone. The receipts were still there, but the drawer now held the cord for an electric jug (something which had appeared from nowhere), a reel of cotton with a pencil pushed through the hole in its centre, and a saucer of orange peel.

"Where's your handbag, Sophie?" Jonny asked.

"My handbag?" Sophie said musingly. "That's right. I was looking for my handbag," she added, suddenly looking very concerned indeed.

The search that followed was long, exhausting and fruitless. There was no sign of the handbag anywhere. Obstinately Jonny went along all the shelves he could find, opened all the cupboards, looked under the chairs and behind cushions and curtains, but without success. He found other things: two oranges hidden behind a cushion, and one of the cats' saucers in the bathroom cupboard. He stood poised over one particular drawer in the desk, frowning at its contents: an old squeezed-out tube of toothpaste, a coat-hanger covered in green and orange crochet, one old-fashioned tin hair-curler, a little glass dish with eggshells in it, a book of needles. Each was innocent enough yet disturbing when they shared the same space and made each other noticeable in an unnatural way. The handbag, though, was not to be found. Jonny did not expect to find it. All the same he searched carefully. Sophie followed him wherever he went, worrying and lamenting.

"My bag," she kept on repeating. "All my *things* are in that bag. Everything! Suppose someone got hold of my post-office savings book? They could take out everything I've got. Everything." It was useless for Jonny to assure her that no one could take out anything from her savings without her signature. Besides, somewhere out there, in the city, possibly in Marribel Road itself, there was a landlord who might know how to forge her signature if necessary. As he searched on, Sophie became more and more agitated.

"Oh dear!" she sighed. "Oh dear, oh dear, oh dear, oh dear!"

In her bedroom, Jonny boldly drew the turquoise fur (a quilt for a double bed, edged with a deep, silk fringe) from the large square object he had noticed earlier, and was enchanted to find a very large, very old television set sitting beneath it.

"I think they should be kept warm," Sophie confided, after looking at it with an astonishment as great as his own. Jonny was glad to see her distracted from the missing handbag.

"Let's take it into the sitting room, shall we?" he suggested. "There isn't enough room in here to swing a cat."

"Oh, I wouldn't do that," said Sophie. "I love those little pussies, I wouldn't do anything to hurt them, not for the world."

"How about a cup of tea?" said Jonny, taking the coward's way out.

"A good idea!" Sophie said warmly, very much as Mrs Einstein might have said to the professor on first hearing him speculate on the unified-field theory.

"I remember just how you like it," she added with the inevitable indulgent twinkle in his direction, and she vanished into the kitchen.

Shifting the set from bedroom to sitting room, Jonny decided to abandon the search for the handbag. He was not sure what to do about it all. Someone was almost certainly enriching himself by calling in every day or two and signing a receipt for whatever Sophie had to give. But Jonny could not quite see himself going to the police with this information. After all, Sophie was unlikely to be a satisfactory witness on her own behalf and, listening to his story, looking at him over an official desk, wouldn't any policeman worth his salt suspect that he, Jonny, was guilty of something himself?

"*How* did you say you met this old lady?" he imagined them asking him, frowning thoughtfully at the face under his bandit hat. "In the early hours of the morning? In a supermarket car park? At three in the morning? I see! And you hadn't met her before? And you went home with her? It's an odd story, isn't it?" There was another inconsistency that also bothered Jonny. There were so many receipts. Spike had been calling for some time, and presumably had had many chances to take Sophie's handbag, so why take it now? After all, wasn't it easier to have Sophie going to the post office every day and bringing back money which could be collected at leisure?

Outside, Marribel Road was darkening, but there was the constant flicker of car lights though the kitchen window. Standing on the balcony of Tap House, Jonny looked at the next-door house. The dummy was gone. It might be all that occupied next-door. There did not seem to be any lights on tonight, nor any sounds of arguments. At least he was sure the handbag existed... was almost sure. When he tried to recall it, he found himself remembering a bag which he knew to be his mother's. The exact size and shape of Sophie's bag remained vague and unsatisfactory, refusing to be recalled.

"Tea!" called Sophie. Jonny went back into the house to be given a cup of hot water and a dubious biscuit, neither of which he wanted. A little later, he made a small dinner for himself and Sophie. It had taken all day, but by now the effects of last night's excesses were largely gone. He had stopped feeling poisoned and had begun to long for chips or a hamburger, or some sort of easy, solid, tasty junk food, with no dishes to do afterwards. The thought of a beer in cheerful company no longer curdled his stomach. He set the table with salt and pepper, and the bowl of oranges. Then Sophie and he sat side by side on the settee and watched television while they ate their dinner. Sophie leaned towards him as if she had a secret to impart.

"They're very good here," she said in a low, intimate voice. "They serve you very nicely."

"Do you come here often?" Jonny asked, and she looked around her room with a puzzled expression.

"I think it does you good to get out every so often," she said. "The food's good, and they're very obliging. Nothing is too much trouble."

Due to some fault in the television every image was shortened and crushed both up and down into an invisible horizon that ran across the middle of the screen. Politicians, trendy announcers, farmers being interviewed on the subject of deer farming were all similarly distorted, drawn towards the intense vanishing line in the centre of the screen, sucked into the heart of things. It was only about two days since Jonny had watched television, but it was like watching it for the first time, for he found he could not easily take his eyes from it. Cars raced and leaped and burned, couples embraced, panels of experts argued, and every now and then exciting atrocities from all over the world were displayed in Sophie's sitting room.

"I don't mind the old black-and-white set," Sophie said smugly.

There had been a terrible earthquake in Central America. People were shown searching and weeping for lost children. But then, a moment later, scenes from a beauty contest filled the screen. A tall, young woman walked towards them, smiling, although Sophie's television set gathered her in and pleated her horizontally across the naval.

"She's not wearing much!" Sophie said, sniggering. "Oh dear, oh dear, oh dear!"

All in all Jonny could not remember a stranger evening, for though it was filled with an expectation he could not explain, he was bored to distraction. He and Sophie sat like bookends with nothing between them that was worth holding up, staring devotedly at the screen, while cats furtively came and went around them. Once, when there were sounds of a terrible cat fight outside, the whole room came alive. All the cats in the room leaped on to the back of the settee and tried to look out of the window.

Sophie had a packet of biscuits hidden under a cushion. Every so often, when she thought he was not looking, she would take out a biscuit and eat it unobtrusively, moving her jaws as little as possible. Once, when Jonny glanced at her, he found she had taken her teeth out and was staring at them with a puzzled expression. He looked away hastily. At last she got up and said very firmly that she was going to bed. She spoke as if they had been arguing about this for a long time, and as though Jonny had been trying to talk her out of it.

"Off you go, Sophie," Jonny said cheerfully, as the announcer said there would be an item from some folk-singer to fill up the two minutes until the next programme was due. "You need your beauty sleep."

Sophie gave him a very severe stare.

"I'm locking my door!" she announced. "Don't think you can get away with anything."

"No," Jonny said. "Lock it tight. Then you won't have to worry."

"I know you mean well," Sophie said relenting, "but there is that streak in your side of the family..."

"Yes, I know. Uncle Bruce," Jonny said.

"Uncle Brian," she corrected him gently.

"That's right!" Jonny agreed. "I just forgot for the moment. I'll watch it, Sophie."

"Oh, you can turn it off whenever you want to," she told him generously, looking at the television set.

"Good night," said Jonny, which was probably the safest thing to say. Sophie went into her room, and a moment later he heard her dragging something across the door.

Stunted figures danced across the screen. It folded them, sucked them in, and then scornfully spat them out again. Jonny watched them fixedly, for in an inscrutable world almost anything could be a clue, if only one had the power to make the right connections.

CHAPTER EIGHT

Once again Jonny woke up in Sophie's house. This time he knew exactly where he was before he opened his eyes. Naked in the rough fleece of blankets, he stared at his striped blazer hanging from the corner of the mantleshelf, at the Walkman further along the shelf, at his jeans slung over the back of the chair. On the floor beside his bed was *A History of Angels,* open at Bonny's name. This morning Jonny thought he could feel her close at hand, mysterious and shadowy, but still inaccessible, and all mixed up with images of pink receipts, missing handbags, the poplar tree beside the river and Nev Fowler.

Nev had leaned so hard against him that Jonny could feel the rough bark of the tree pressing into his back even through his school jersey. Nev's bony knees dug into his thighs. The chilly blade of the knife lay against his throat. Nev stared down into Jonny's eyes with a curious expression, antagonistic, but fascinated as well. "If you tell anyone about this, I'll kill you," Nev promised in his high-pitched voice.*

"You can try," Jonny said aloud, smiling and looking happy in the dusty bedroom of Sophie's house. He was going to have to get up and face another day.

"Are you the sheep God wants you to be?" Jonny asked himself, getting out of bed. He could not remember ever having longed for fresh clothes as much as he longed for them now, looking at the brown patches of dried blood on the front of his shirt.

Shaking his head, he padded down to the bathroom, brushed his teeth with his new toothbrush, and studied his face critically. One eye, held in a rich bracket of indigo, looked as if it might have been put in as an afterthought. Other bruises were turning to streaks of yellow and green.

"Somewhere over the rainbow," Jonny sang to his reflection. He looked disreputable, not only bruised but needing a shave. However, he had no razor. He wondered about having a bath, but there were no clean clothes to change into, so he decided to postpone it until later in the day when he would surely be home again. With that he thought uneasily about his mother who might be worrying at his absence by now. All the same, he hid his new toothbrush in case Sophie found it and put it to some terrible use, before he went out on to the landing, opened the sitting-room door and peered through.

The curtains were still drawn across; the room was filled with the sort of light that made it seem earlier in the morning than it really was. Something scarlet – squashed and shapeless – was squatting on the table. For a moment he thought one of the cats had had a horrid accident and had climbed on to the table to die. Then he saw that it was Sophie's handbag which had reappeared quite inexplicably. Jonny stared at it, mystified, and then advanced a step into the room, but something muttered and scrambled at knee level in front of him, and when he made out what it was Jonny forgot the handbag, miraculously restored though it was, and flung himself backwards through the door on to the landing, slamming the door behind him and flattening himself against the wall, just like the detective in a thriller. For the first time in years he found himself blushing. The uneasy heat even crawled in under his hair.

On the other side of the door Sophie scrambled like a dog down on all fours, head bent towards the floor, naked except for her pot hat and unravelling singlet. He had only had one look, but he had the oddest impression that she had a sleek rat's tail trailing behind her.

"Oh dear, oh dear, oh dear," she had been muttering to herself. "Oh dear, oh dear, oh dear!"

Over the last few years Jonny had seen many pictures of naked women in films, magazines, and photographs shown round at school. He had even seen one or two real live girls. He had believed that female nakedness could never embarrass him, but now he realised it depended on the age of the woman. One mere glance at Sophie's bare bottom and he was outraged. I don't have to put up with this, he thought angrily, as if Sophie had played a malicious trick on him.

From several steps below him a tabby cat looked at him contemptuously, then stuck its hind leg competently up in the air and began to wash its own tail. The cat was so self-possessed, so capable, that it reproached Jonny's confusion. He began to wonder if Sophie had had a fall or had possibly hurt herself in any way. Opening the door very cautiously he peered in again, wondering just what was going on without looking at Sophie too directly. The rat's tail was the cord of the toaster which Sophie had been pulling across the floor after her. Now she was trying to force the plug into a wall socket, holding it upside down and jabbing viciously at the wall, furious because it would not fit. She looked as if she were trying to kill something small but tough. Jonny thought she was running terrible risks and, half expecting to see electricity leap out and savage her at any moment, decided to intervene.

"Sophie!" he shouted, and she jumped convulsively. "Stop that! It's dangerous."

"Well, this thing that I'm supposed to get my heat from," she cried piteously, "won't work." Just beyond her the heater sat, totally ignored. "Errol used to fix everything for me," she added, "but I don't know where he is."

"You're trying to plug the wrong thing in," Jonny said impatiently, maddened by the impossibility of it all. "Errol's dead. There's only me." She had frightened him.

His voice sounded brutal in his own ears, and he was alarmed all over again to hear himself saying, "There's only me," for it was true, and he hated the thought of it. Now she held out her hand to him, needing to be steadied as she got to her feet again. Jonny took it without hesitation.

Five years ago he, too, had held out his hand after scrambling up the slope, leaving the wicked edge from which he had seen his sister's body lying among the serpents of foam. They'll blame me, he had thought despairingly, for, particularly over the last few months, Janine had blamed him for everything, and his parents seldom argued with her. "Don't upset Janine," they had warned him over and over again. Jonny had held up his hand to Bonny who leaned down from under the danger sign to meet him. "Oh, Jonny!" she had said. "I thought you'd fall too." A little later, seeing him shaking and gibbering like a frightened monkey she had suddenly cried, "Don't! Don't!" And, although he was a boy of fourteen, she had put her arms around him as if he were small again. He had found that she was trembling too, a vibration in phase with his own; had felt and remembered (though he afterwards felt rather guilty for noticing such a thing at such a time) the warmth of her honey-coloured skin and the swell of her breasts, the slow change of which he had watched secretly over the last three years, "Was it my fault?" he had cried. "They'll blame me." "Don't tell them," she advised. "Say you were up here with me." It was her last advice as Pythoness.

Only a few minutes later she was to throw her snake ring away. Off it went, the snake with its tail in its mouth, spinning in the last of the evening sunshine.

But this time it was Sophie putting up her hand, and Jonny's turn to be rescuer. No doubt the world was full of hands being held out, one way or another, and once your own had been taken, you were obliged to pass the help on. So now Jonny hauled Sophie to her feet. She was surprisingly heavy for someone so thin.

"Errol dead?" she cried in astonishment rather than grief. "I'm glad you told me that. I ought to be told these things. Those people next door – they keep me in the dark about everything." But then her first expression of surprise altered and she grew sombre and remote. Her hands, still grasping Jonny's, were very knobbly. He wondered if she had arthritis – if holding things actually hurt her – and looked with dismay at her forearm, so shrunken around its core of bone it was no larger than the round shiny arms the twins sometimes put around his neck.

"He was a good husband, you know," Sophie went on musingly, staring at Jonny intently, apparently trying to fix the fading image of Errol beyond all chance of loss. "I've never forgotten *you*," she added apologetically, "but Errol was one of nature's gentlemen."

"Oh, God, Sophie, put something on!" begged Jonny. "Be one of nature's ladies. You'll freeze."

The closeness of her old skin and bone filled him with a repulsion that was not far from being fear, and which felt like an instinct, too natural to be denied, although he was ashamed of feeling it. Besides, even in her unravelling singlet and pot hat, Sophie still somehow managed to be genteel.

"I'll find your clothes," Jonny cried, taking off his blazer and draping it around her. He dived into her bedroom and searched in a flustered way, but yesterday's clothes had vanished as though they had never existed. Jonny began to believe that there was a science-fiction space in Sophie's house, some sort of crack between the dimensions perhaps, into which an absent-minded old lady might pop her handbag or her clothes.

Sophie watched him from the doorway, frowning as darkly as anyone with next to no eyebrows could be expected to frown. Her disapproving look caused Jonny to say crossly, "I don't want to do this, you know. Where are your clothes?"

"It's not very nice," said Sophie, ignoring his question, "to have someone touching your things."

"I don't *want* to touch them!" Jonny snapped. "But look at you: standing around getting cold. I wouldn't let my little sisters stand around like that."

"You haven't *got* any sisters," Sophie said. "I know all your family."

Her wardrobe, packed with clothes – blouses, dresses, various shabby coats – looked impenetrable.

"Those are *my* clothes," Sophie said. "I don't think any of them will fit you."

Jonny was suddenly inspired.

"Look! Why don't you have a bath?" he asked. "I mean it wouldn't be any more trouble, would it? And you sure as hell *need* one." And, without waiting for her to argue, he swept past her to the bathroom and turned on the taps. Water, heavily stained with rust, gushed out vigorously. The taps had obviously not been turned on for a long time. However, as Jonny looked at it gloomily, the water slowly cleared. It was plentiful and hot, a tribute no doubt to the vanished skill of Errol. On top of the bathroom cupboard, next to his toothbrush, a dusty jar of bath salts caught Jonny's eye. Quickly, he emptied about a quarter of the bottle into the bath, overwhelming the traces of rust with brilliant green. A scented, viridian foam rose around the yellowing porcelain.

Sophie, flamboyant in his blazer, followed him into the bathroom and looked at the green water. Her truculent expression changed at the sight of the bubbles, giving way to one of soft enchantment.

"It *is* prettty, isn't it?" she cried enthusiastically.

"Dive right in, Sophie," Jonny said. "It's all yours."

"*You* can have half of it," said Sophie generously, giving him an indulgent smile.

"You have it all," said Jonny quickly. "Go on! Hop in! I won't look. I'll sort out some clothes for you," he added.

But Sophie merely dabbled her fingers in the water and said it was too hot. Jonny tested it himself, and looked at her severely.

"It is not too hot," he declared. "It's lukewarm. Go on! No putting it off." As he spoke, he understood that it was not the temperature that was putting her off, but the high sides of the bath, and that she needed assistance which only he could give. Jonny breathed out in a great noisy groan which turned into a giggle at the end. Then he laughed.

"Oh, well, why not?" he said aloud. "Things can't get any worse." He held out his hand. "Here, Missus, one, two, three!"

Timorously pointing her bumpy toes, Sophie stepped into the bath, holding Jonny's hand rather high as if she were dancing a minuet with him. Paddling in the green water, she turned to him and said in a formal way, "I thank you very much," still holding his right hand daintily. Jonny smiled a little and swept his left hand sideways in an accommodating acknowledgement. Only when she was safely squatting among green bubbles did she release her anxious grasp on his fingers.

"That's just about right!" she said, splashing the water as the edge of her grey singlet billowed out around her.

"Come on! Let's skin the rabbit," Jonny said, which was what his father used to say when he and Janine were tiny and getting undressed in front of the fire. Pulling off

Sophie's singlet, Jonny felt an unexpected warmth for his father. Though his confused concern often expressed itself in criticism and anger these days, he had been kind and reassuring when Jonny was small. It was little children he liked, not large, bewildered sons. Keys hung around Sophie's neck on their bit of string. Jonny removed them carefully, and put them in a soap-dish by the hand-basin.

Yesterday, he had restored three cakes of soap to the bathroom, but since then, during that active time in the late afternoon, Sophie must have tidied them somewhere else. After a moment's thought he went to the kitchen where he found one of them in a saucer in the fridge. He took it back to her with a facecloth and the cleanest towel that he could find.

"Wash all over," he told her, like a stern father. "Behind your ears! Everywhere!" Then he left her to it.

Once out of the bathroom he flopped down in a chair, feeling he had already done a hard day's work. For perhaps two minutes he sat there, eyes closed. Then he leaped up, drew the curtains back, opened the windows and recommenced the search for clothes. Once in Sophie's bedroom he was seized yet again by the wish to bring some sort of order to chaos. At home he was regarded as the source of disorder. Here, things were reversed. In Sophie's house *he* was the one who tidied up, who knew where to find things. So he carried, first her blankets and sheets, and then her mattress, out on to the balcony. It wasn't until he was leaning the mattress against the balcony rail that he realised there was a wet patch on it, more or less the same shape as Africa. For a moment it seemed about the same size.

Jonny leaned back against the balcony rail and stared severely at the patch which refused to go away. He ran his hands into his hair in an ancient gesture of despair, and then looked up at the sky checking the weather which he had had no time to notice until now. The day around him was pleasant but not particularly hot. The mattress would certainly not dry quickly. After some thought he turned it over, but the wetness went right through, though on the other side it looked more like South America. Continental drift, though Jonny, picking up the corner of the electric blanket gingerly even though it wasn't plugged in. It was not only wet but worn in places. The unseen assassin of Sophie's house stalked her, even in bed.

At last, deciding that street air, even with residues of lead, could only be good for this bedding, he left it on the balcony and went to find possible clothes, selecting a striped skirt and a viyella blouse whose dense patterns somehow absorbed the worst of the stains. Searching for clean underwear, he opened a drawer in the oak dressing-table with its wide tilted mirror, and found it full of strange, knitted clothes, bed jackets, shrunken jerseys, singlets so small and matted it was hard to believe that even Sophie could fit into them, and voluminous pants with elastic in the legs. Rummaging around looking for something reasonably clean and wearable, Jonny suddenly found himself holding a twenty-dollar note. He had come on a hoard of about a hundred and twenty dollars, some of which was folded up in a bloodstained handkerchief. Jonny straightened, flicking the money through his fingers.

I could pay myself for helping her into the bath, he thought, or I could just take it. No one would know.

"Sophie," he called out, counting the money again. "Are you all right?" Each time he counted the money it seemed more like his money than Sophie's.

"Yes," she called back from the bathroom. "I'm quite clean."

In the end Jonny pushed the money back under the misshapen clothes. There was no great elation in overcoming this particular temptation. I'm mad, Jonny thought as he made for the bathroom door. That money's just wasted. He banged on the bathroom door.

"Are you decent?" he called, for though he knew she couldn't be, it seemed fair to warn her that he was coming.

"I don't know," she said doubtfully, as if he had asked her a particularly difficult riddle. Jonny came into a room smelling powerfully of bath salts, put Sophie's clothes on the closed lid of the lavatory and, averting his eyes slightly, helped her out of the bath in the same courtly way he had helped her into it.

"You're very good," Sophie said graciously.

"We'd go well in the tango, Soph," Jonny said, dropping the string of keys around her neck, and wrapping her hastily in a towel.

"I like the old-fashioned dances," Sophie confided. "Errol was a good dancer, you know. He liked the foxtrot."

"I'll bet," Jonny said, laughing. Sophie laughed too, copying him. They looked into one another's eyes, Sophie quite as innocent but not quite as sexless as the twins (though these days even they would sometimes cover themselves with their towels and cry, "Don't look!"). Jonny showed Sophie her clothes and fled to the kitchen thinking he would get breakfast. He had barely begun to search for the bread when there was a thump and a cry. Jonny wheeled around.

"Sophie! Sophie! Are you all right?" he shouted.

"Oh, it *is* sore!" she moaned. Gritting his teeth and swearing through them, Jonny charged back into the bathroom to find her sitting on the floor, her pants twisted around her ankles.

"Well, you *have* got your knickers in a twist," Jonny said. "How on earth would you get on without me?" The words rang in his ears like alarm bells.

"I sat down rather hard," Sophie complained, wincing and trying to rub the pain away as little children do. She did not even try to be brave. "Oh, it's so sore," she groaned.

"Well, there you are," Jonny said, shaking the pants out. "You shouldn't wear such – such big ones."

"I don't like them tight," Sophie said, holding her hand up to him once more. She placed her hand on his bent back to steady herself as he held the pants for her to get into.

"Look, Sophie, I'm warning you," Jonny said. "Be careful, because after this you're on your own. You don't want me to dress you, do you? Not with me taking after Uncle Brian and all that."

"Oh, no," she said in a shocked voice, but then spoiled it by giving a naughty chuckle as he left the room.

"What have I come down to?" Jonny asked himself as he peeled an orange and cut it into quarters for her. Over the past year and a half he had developed the reputation, among his parents' friends, of being bad, mad and dangerous to know, and though he was often surprised when people acted as if they believed it, he was flattered too. He did not want to turn into the sort of man who worried over wet mattresses, baths and breakfasts; he hated the heavy, harassed feeling that possessed him. Sophie's house felt like a trap closing around him.

I've got to get out of here, he thought.

Twice he had been on the point of leaving Sophie's house. Twice something happened to stop him. More and more it was becoming *his* job to look after Sophie, his job and his alone to save her from malnutrition, from dirt and danger, even from her own menacing house. She might be zapped by electricity, trip over a cat, fall on her worn carpet and crack her head open. Transfixed, Jonny had a vision of her lying at the foot of her stairs with the very last of her memory seeping out through the crack in her skull, barely staining the wood as it soaked away for ever. There wouldn't be much mess, there was so little memory left in there. Jonny began buttering bread, so blinded by this image that he nearly cut his finger.

I've just got to get out of here, he thought again. To hell with it!

But she's a *sign*, said another part of his mind. You have to go with the signs. Jonny had always been willingly influenced by the signs and hated to see them treated carelessly. A week after Janine's death he had gone back to the reserve, had recalled the bright trajectory of the serpent ring and searched for it over several afternoons...

Jonny dragged his thoughts back to Sophie, understanding now that getting dressed was a major accomplishment for her, and that she was dirty because it was safer to be dirty. Jonny danced on the kitchen floor, looking down at his clever feet which still knew what they could do and did it without thinking.

"Chick-chick-chick-chick-chicken!" he sang to them softly, understanding, too, that their skill was only a temporary gift which would be called in one day. Sophie, coming back into the kitchen, respectably dressed, looked at him in surprise.

"I haven't got any of those thingummies," she said. "You know, the things that go on your legs." Jonny supposed she meant stockings.

"Forget the thingummies and just think about the whatsitsnames," he told her, showing her her breakfast. Her whole face lit up with pleasure.

"That does look nice," she said. "You're very good to me."

"I could be better," Jonny replied, but she looked up at him with her indulgent smile.

"You're good enough for me," she said, reassuring him.

As she ate her breakfast, Jonny put the mattress back on her bed, and covered the wet patches with plastic bin-liners. All the sheets in the kitchen cupboard were full of holes, but he chose the best he could find and made her bed up for her. Then he went upstairs, put on his hat, hung the Walkman at his belt, hooked the headphones round his neck, and patted the tapes and wallet in his pocket, sternly driving out thoughts of the easy riches hidden around the house. He decided to leave the toothbrush as an odd sort of memorial to his fleeting presence in the house. His last act of housekeeping was to make Sophie a real cup of tea. The milk was missing from the fridge but he quickly located it in another cupboard among two large piles of saucers.

"I'll get *you* one," Sophie said eagerly as he placed the cup of tea in front of her.

"Later," Jonny said, a little guiltily, and then said her name seriously, so that she looked up at him questioningly, her mouth bulging with bread. "Nothing!" he exclaimed with a sigh. "Just – you know – steady as you go, and all that." He went past her to the door and out on to the landing, then ran lightly down the stairs, watched by a selection of cats, all smiling cynically under their whiskers. They knew him for a deserter.

There must be someone who looks after people like Sophie, Jonny thought, suddenly inspired, someone who would do it as a proper job, and Sophie could afford help. He had read about an Old People's Council, or something similar. His conscience relaxed. I didn't take that money, he reminded it. I could have.

Jonny took hold of the door handle, turned it, stepped out on to the pavement and then hesitated before he closed it behind him, staring back at the stairs with irritated puzzlement. Come on, he told himself, get it over and done with and shut the door firmly. He was outside the house, and now must escape its field by putting distance between himself and the door so it could not draw him back again.

"Act casual!" he said aloud. He stretched a little, yawned and then made off lazily in the direction of the post office. Walking on his own up the one-way street, against the flow of the traffic, might break the spell of Sophie's house, like going anticlockwise around a church –

or was it clockwise? He must have guessed right for nothing happened to stop him. No one spoke his name. He was walking away, carrying everything he had brought with him. Every moment saw him closer and closer to freedom.

CHAPTER NINE

Although he began by walking off very firmly, as if he and Sophie's house had nothing to do with one another, Jonny stopped at the railway line and looked nervously back over his shoulder.

On this particular morning, and from this distance, it was just an old house, remarkable only for the tap, and even that was a mere ornament, worth a smile and nothing more. Beyond it, he could catch a glimpse of its sister house with an empty balcony. All sense of displacement, all feeling that he was living, bewitched, in a replica of the real city was gone.

Jonny with filled with great relief. He could have danced. He *did* dance, going forward in a series of silent heel and toe taps, filling in the sound in his own mind, building up a pattern of single, double and triple beats. People in cars joining the long line at a red light stared at him, unsmiling. Jonny, dancing harder, waved both arms at his audience and left them behind, moving onwards in a series of stifled bombashays on to the shingle by the railway line. The ordinariness of everything delighted him. He was dancing his way out of a perverse enchantment, for Sophie's house, with its tribe of cats and its dirt and anarchy, was falling away behind him.

After all, if it turned out to be really important he would search for Bonny in an organised way, using common sense. Meanwhile, he could return to living an ordinary life – be a man, and not a divining rod twisting towards revelation. Somewhere, only a few miles away, there was a proper house under proper control – a house which would welcome him back – a house with two little sisters, one dog, one cat, and cheese in the fridge, not in the soap-dish. And if for a couple of crazy days he had made use of Sophie's house – well, at least he had left it cleaner, tidier and stocked with food. All sorts of possibilities passed through his head. In this mood there was no end to what he might achieve.

"I'll get a job," he told himself. "I'll do anything – *anything*. I'll just apply for whatever's going!"

And yet, for a moment, crossing the railway line, keeping his eye on a white van rattling past him, his purposeful steps faltered as he wondered whether or not one was entitled to turn away from the wheel of fortune because its magical accidents offered something one didn't want to get mixed up with? (There had been three people in the van, he thought, but street reflections sliding across the windscreen had prevented him from seeing their faces. Nevertheless...)

Coming down the street towards him was a delicious smell. He knew at once what it was. It was toasted sandwiches; it was chips. The old pub, The Colville, had opened its doors. His escape was established; he was free, and the yearning for ordinary, vulgar food possessed him fiercely. Jonny decided he had all day ahead of him. He could celebrate his return to real life. Crossing the road he went into the public bar. It was almost empty at this time of day and he looked at it with pleasure, for it was all very basic – no stained glass or tasteful carpeting – nothing to attract young executives and their wives. Behind the counter the bar glittered like a pantomime stage, promising pleasure and transformation. A mirror behind the bottles multiplied them into a cast of thousands. A card advertised toasted sandwiches and bar lunches. A barman stood behind the counter, beer-gun levelled into a tankard. Jonny had a moment of a Western fantasy. (Peter drew low and fired. Pow! Struck by the amber shaft, Demon Thirst fell, mortally wounded. No one faster on the draw than Beer-gun Pete!)

Sunshine coming through the window touched the handles of lager so that they seemed to brim over with pure gold. Still, Jonny's light-hearted exhilaration at escaping from the crazy field of Sophie's house was still crossed with good intentions for the immediate future. He was determined to be careful. He felt powerful simply going up to the bar and ordering lemonade, just like an old-fashioned cowboy hero. Here, in The Colville pub, the golden West reigned supreme. Jonny carried a glass and his bottle of lemonade over to a corner table and toasted his own return to everyday life. In due course he was called over to collect his order of chips and a toasted cheese-sandwich from the counter, where the barman, having no other customer to distract him, leaned on the counter reading a yachting magazine. Jonny carried his tray back to the table. He enjoyed merely holding the chips which were light and crisp and salty – the first serving of the day. Someone had left a paper on the table, and he picked it up, noted with satisfaction the normal acrimonious discussions about city rates and pollution of the river, the saga of Hinerangi Hotene (still at large), the closure of one big city firm and the take-over of another. But as he ate the last chip, concentrating on the sharpness of the salt and the blandness of the potato, the barman absent-mindedly reached over and turned on a transistor radio that stood beside the till, and the bar rang with abrupt music. It was a song by the very band whose tape was in Jonny's Walkman, but of course this time its statements were public ones.

Jonny, standing up to leave, was so surprised that he had to touch his headphones to make sure they were around his neck and not over his ears. He had almost come to believe that those voices were intended for him alone, and so they were – in Sophie's house.

"WE'VE COME TO TAKE YOU HOME," sang the band, which should have been reassuring but actually sounded ominous. Jonny glanced over towards the little radio, smiling ruefully, and then, in the very act of taking a step towards the door, stopped and stared. Something inside him tightened up; he could feel his expression grow threatening.

"LET'S HIT THE TRACK," sang the band, but Jonny wasn't consciously aware of hearing it. He simply stared at the cream-coloured transistor by the till and, when he moved at last, it was not towards the door after all. Like a doomed hero he went over to the counter instead, and put money down for another bottle of lemonade. As the barman turned to get it, Jonny picked up the transistor and turned it casually over and over.

"Where did you get this?" he asked trying to sound offhand and slightly scornful. Instead he heard the words come out accusingly.

It felt exactly like Sophie's radio, light and trashy, as frail in its plastic case as its owner under her unravelling singlet. He had checked on her hidden money and had searched for her handbag, but he had forgotten all about the radio until now.

"Got it last night," the barman said. "For the kids. I forgot to take it home." He was a little ashamed of the lady-like cream plastic case with its touches of gold. "It sounds all right with new batteries, doesn't it?"

"Last night?" Jonny cried. "Who'd you get it from?" His voice still sounded unduly sharp, and the barman looked at him suspiciously.

"Who's asking?" he asked in turn.

"I was just curious," said Jonny, forcing himself into sounding casual. "That's all. It's an old model. It – it looks like one my granny used to have."

The barman flicked the top off the lemonade bottle and slid it over to him, but he volunteered no further information. Jonny tried again.

"Did you get it locally?"

"Traded it for a jug of beer," the barman said. "It's not worth anything."

"Mind you – taking a risk, weren't you?" Jonny suggested. "Trading under the counter?"

"Are you a cop?" asked the barman, and Jonny grinned.

"God, no! Do I look like it?" he asked derisively.

"You can't always go by looks," said the barman. "They have to take all sorts these days."

"Gee, thanks!" Jonny said. He was sure it was Sophie's radio, but proof was another matter, and he could hardly produce Sophie as a witness. All the same the appearance of the radio here, the renewed certainty that someone was preying on Sophie, as he had been tempted to do himself, banished his new-born and fragile exhilaration. As he picked up the lemonade and went back to his table the barman called from behind him.

"I know the bloke I bought it from. He's always in here."

Jonny nodded, and held up his hands miming surrender. The bottle was in his right hand. He nearly spilt lemonade all over himself.

People suddenly started to come into the bar. Within a few minutes it had become quite crowded. Jonny looked at his watch. It was half-past eleven – perhaps an early lunch-hour for people working at *Industrial Gloves*, or *Plastic Fabrications,* or *Cognito Systems* or any other of the factories and offices that were slowly taking over the whole suburb of Colville. They were ordering food and bottles of beer or glasses of wine. The tables slowly filled. Others got chips and sandwiches as take-aways and headed out again.

Jonny sat with his hands on either side of his head. Supposing he went to the police and said that Sophie was being robbed, and supposing they believed him: what could they do? Put a guard around Sophie's house? Sophie was more likely to complain about policemen questioning her than about the missing radio. Could you put in a complaint on another person's behalf? Surely there must be someone he could go to, someone who could tell him just whose job it was to look after Sophie.

As he brooded on matters like these, a shadow slid across the table, for someone was moving past the pub window towards his table, someone who came to a standstill, waited to be noticed, and spoke at last.

"Geez! It's Chicken Dart, isn't it?" cried the voice after a moment. It sounded astonished, but the speaker was only acting astonishment.

Jonny recognised that shrewd, confident accent immediately. Looking up, he found himself staring straight at a wiry young man, slightly older and taller than he was, with a wide, craggy forehead beetling out over lively, hazel eyes, a narrow jaw, and a soft, full-lipped mouth. The newcomer's hair stood up in flamboyant locks. They were all the more noticeable because the sides of his head were shaved so that the hair on the crown, left to grow rather long, looked like a blond fountain. There, before him, was Nev Fowler, the nemesis of his Colville schooldays, and though this time round it was Nev whose hair was dyed, while Jonny's was its natural brown, Nev was still Nev, and already making it plain that he believed Jonny was still the dancing Chickenbits boy and a natural victim.

CHAPTER TEN

"Share a bottle?" offered Nev, flourishing a bottle of beer, rather as Sophie had flourished a milk bottle the previous day. "For old times' sake," he added with a smile – sly, confiding, yet shame-faced, acknowledging a fault long past and expecting to be forgiven.

But Nev could be nice when he wanted to – he even had a sense of humour. Though Jonny had never had any benefit from it himself, he remembered seeing other people, including teachers, respond to it. As he smiled back he felt a twitch of old, left-over terror, as people who have lost a leg are said to be able to feel the itching of toes they no longer have. But it didn't last. The memory of Nev was more frightening than the real man.

Since their last meeting, years ago, Nev had grown even taller and stronger, but Jonny had changed too, in ways that it would be hard for Nev to guess at. Of course, some things don't change. Nev still had a high-pitched voice even though his voice had broken since Jonny heard it last, and he still looked as if his parents had carefully constructed him out of the best bits of earlier experimental models. He wasn't bad-looking, but there was something slightly disproportionate about him. It wouldn't have been surprising to see a bolt at his temple and stitches across his forehead or around his wrists. Yet, here in The Colville pub, he seemed younger than he had ever seemed at school where he had always looked older and more knowing than anyone else, even the teachers. His cunning was still there, easy to see, but by now other people had caught up on him and it didn't show as much as it used to.

Certainly, meeting him like this, no one would suspect that he could be merciless. The grin he gave Jonny was unexpectedly pleasant, and it wasn't the only unexpected thing about him, although it took Jonny a minute or two to work out just what it was that was different. Then he realised he had never seen Nev getting around on his own. He had always had a gang with him, not because he ever needed help, but because he liked applause. That was the one thing Nev and Janine had had in common. Jonny looked casually around the room. Beyond the beer bottle he saw that a table which had been empty was now occupied by two other young men, both staring at him very intently. When they saw he had noticed them, they turned away and began to talk to each other.

"Gee, thanks, Nev – actually I was just on my way," Jonny said.

"Actually, you were sitting there dreaming your head off," Nev said. "I've been keeping tabs on you. Same old Chickie!" His first smile had sharpened. He sat down beside Jonny quite confidently, for he was in his own place, and whether Jonny wanted to share the table or not didn't matter at all. "Long time no see, Chickie!"

"It has been a while," Jonny agreed.

"Well, you lot moved away to Seacliff, didn't you?" Nev went on. Jonny nodded, though Nev was not really asking him anything. "Nice area!" Nev said in tones of exaggerated respect, waiting for Jonny to comment, but Jonny remained silent.

"SILENCE IS GOLDEN – WORDS FALL LIKE STONES," the band sang to him, but only out of memory.

"I've never moved myself," Nev went on. His sarcastic voice changed almost immediately, grew contemplative, reminiscent. "I know this place like the back of my hand. It's like inheriting one of those estates, really. This pub here, for example, this pub... Well, my mother's brother is the licensee." He paused, watching Jonny closely for any suggestion that, as a resident of Seacliff, he might be thinking poorly of Colville. Jonny shrugged. Nev lay back in his chair, tilted it at an angle, then swung his feet in new boots on to the table. The boots occupied table space which Nev could fairly regard as his own, yet somehow it was impossible for Jonny to look around them. Unless he deliberately turned away he was forced to consider the boots. "One of my other uncles is a councillor now," Nev went on. "My family really run Colville. I do deliveries for my cousin... do you remember my cousin with the hardware shop? Transport goes with the job."

His boots were hand-sewn, embossed-leather cowboy boots which had had metal tips moulded around the toes.

"I've never wanted to leave," he added.

"Great," said Jonny heartily. "Sounds as if you're doing well."

Nev's eyes were moving restlessly the whole time, flickering around the room, from floor to ceiling, from counter to door, recording everyone who came in, everyone who went out, glancing from the barman behind the counter to his friends sitting at their own table, but always returning to Jonny with unwilling curiosity, no doubt recording his hair, his bruises, his Walkman, and every stripe on his blazer.

"I've been keeping an eye on you," Nev went on casually. "I knew you were back."

"Yes, but you'll need to get the exhaust of that van fixed if you want to sneak up on me," Jonny answered.

A shadow of annoyance passed over Nev's face. He reached down and picked up the bottle from beside his chair.

"It was you in the car park the other night, wasn't it?" he asked. "Not that I exactly recognised you, but that jacket's a giveaway, isn't it? The next thing, there you were outside the post office with old lady West, and then later you were dancing down by the river… Same old Chickie, I thought. Looking for trouble."

"It's not hard to find," Jonny said. "There's plenty for everyone." But if Nev understood that this was a warning, he did not show it. A narrow collar of foam rose about the edge of his glass, but none of the beer flowed down the side. Nev stopped pouring with a flourish, giving the bottle a professional little twist before setting it down on the floor again.

"I nearly stopped the van and had a word with you then," Nev said. "Force of habit, I suppose. Then I thought, 'Live and let live.'" Jonny laughed. "What's the joke?" Nev asked, looking up sharply.

"It must have been a shock to your system – having a thought like that," Jonny said.

Nev lifted his glass towards Jonny as if toasting him, but it was the old, threatening Nev that looked over the foam at him. If Janine had been friendly to Nev, he might have been kinder to Jonny, might even have taken his side in playground arguments. With his hair bleached white, Jonny had rather resembled Janine, and it suddenly occurred to him that when Nev had leaned against him, staring at him so very intently, he might have been trying to imagine that it was Janine he had, trapped and helpless, against the poplar tree.

"So where do you hang out?" Nev asked casually. Jonny did not want to give Nev any information he did not already have.

"I've just been visiting," he said. "I don't live here."

"I wouldn't have thought you'd want to come back again," Nev commented. "Not you!"

"It's surprising what you get homesick for," Jonny said vaguely.

"Anyhow, you lot always thought you were a bit too good for the rest of us," Nev went on, probably remembering Janine's ruthless remarks about Colville. It was strange how Nev had always seemed to like the very things in Janine that he hated most in Jonny – pale, shining hair, dancing, and fame – and certainly Janine was capable of being just as merciless in her way as Nev was in his.

"So what are you doing these days?" Nev persisted, a little puzzled by Jonny's refusal to say more than he absolutely had to.

"Nothing much... I'm on the dole," Jonny said.

Satisfaction brightened Nev's expression.

"*I've* worked ever since I left school," he said. "I've never been out of work, not once."

"Good on you," Jonny said laconically. A disquieting thought had come to him. Perhaps, after all, he was still in the power of Sophie's house. He had imagined he was escaping, but really he was just being given a bit of extra latitude.

Realising he had lost Jonny's full attention, Nev suddenly sat up, picked up his bottle and gestured towards Jonny's empty glass.

"Top you up?" he offered, and poured beer into the glass without waiting for Jonny to say either yes or no. "Drink up, Chickie," he said. "It'll make a man of you."

A little silence fell. For the first time since finding himself in unwelcome company Jonny looked directly into Nev's eyes, lifting the glass as he did so. Nev returned Jonny's gaze almost as steadily as if he were an honest man, but there was a little flicker of uncertainty before he looked away, saying, "So, who's beating you up these days, Chickie? Someone is."

"My mother," Jonny replied, still considering whether or not he should take exception to a certain insolent implication in Nev's last comment. It was not a new insult. In the past, when he was still a tap-dancer, the boys had cried derisively, "What *are* you, Dart?" Only two nights ago he had taken violent exception to a similar suggestion. With astonishment he saw that his careless reply, made without any particular thought of insult or aggravation, had stung Nev with its very carelessness. Perhaps since beating up people was a talent of Nev's, it was tactless to joke about it.

"You always made bloody smart remarks, that's the trouble with you, Chickie," said Nev. His lumpy forehead appeared to settle down even lower over the eyes, squashing them into slits and intensifying the hazel stare. "I hate that."

Jonny, who had once seen this face only an inch away from his own, and had felt the cold blade of the sheath knife pressed against his throat, had imagined that every mark, every mole, every hair, even the texture of Nev's skin would be fixed in his memory for ever, but after all he had forgotten that odd, lowering effect. This time, however, he could not be frightened. He just laughed and drank some of the beer. Nev drank too, then frowned and thumped his glass down.

"So you want to buy a cheap transistor radio," he said.

Until that moment Jonny had not associated Nev's presence at his table with the questions he had asked the barman. Nev had seemed too much like someone from an entirely different life. Involuntarily he glanced back towards the bar and realised that they were under observation.

Sometimes, from within, Jonny felt himself grow alarming, felt his teeth clench, his eyes grow round like the eyes of a bird of prey, the corners of his mouth drag down. At such moments he easily melted into fury with pleasure, lost all doubts and hesitations, enjoying the singleness of simple rage. "You look terrific – like a demon," a girl had once told him. But Jonny did not want Nev to see this demon at this particular moment, so looked down, casually buttoning and then unbuttoning the top of his blazer.

"Barry said you were asking..." Nev's voice went on. "Barry – that's Barry behind the bar – Barry and I are old mates. I do him a favour or two, and I don't mind doing one for you, Chickie, but go easy on the smart remarks."

Jonny felt his blinding moment of fury had come and gone unseen, and looked up at Nev over the table. Some trace of it, however, must have remained, for Nev paused before repeating rather more slowly. "Barry said you asked him."

"I was just curious," Jonny said in a bored voice. "My aunt used to have a model just like that."

"You don't want one yourself, then?" asked Nev. "Not that I could get one exactly the same but..."

"Where did you get that one?" Jonny had meant his question to be casual, but it came out loaded with scornful implication. Nev's flickering gaze stopped flickering. Directed exclusively at Jonny, it lay against him like cold steel.

"Someone I'd done a good turn to gave it to me," he said. He glanced back at the table where the other young men sat. Jonny looked, too. One met Jonny's eyes and looked away at once, but the other, a weedy boy, stared back unblinkingly. Nev persisted.

"Barry said you wanted to know where it came from. So – what's it to you, Chickie? Go on. Tell me! I might be able to do you a good turn some day."

Jonny got to his feet.

"You wouldn't know a good turn if you fell over one," he said. "Well, nice meeting you, Nev. Steady as you go."

Nev was reluctant to let him escape.

"Hang on a moment..." he said. "Your sister – what was her name...?" He paused.

"Janine," Jonny answered.

"Yeah – Janine – that's right! She wrote herself off, didn't she? So who's looking after you now?"

"I get by," Jonny replied, pushing his hands into his pockets. A cold slither of steel inserted itself between his fingers. It was the key to Sophie's house. "I take each day as it comes," he added, insulting Nev by looking inward and not outward, by showing his old enemy that he could be preoccupied with other even more important things in Nev's company.

"Me, too," was all Nev said. "I take each day as it comes, too."

"Is that all you take?" Jonny asked him. He did a slap-up on one foot, then a slap-up and change with the other, finishing with a ballstep. "This step's called a grab-off, Nev. Ever heard of a grab-off?" Without the proper shoes his dancing feet made no sound except in his own mind, but of course Nev knew he was being insolent.

"Oh, Chickie... You watch it..." he began, shaking his head, but Jonny interrupted him.

"If I was you, I'd really get the most out of Colville while you can," he said. "It's melting away out there." He left the pub without looking back at Nev, but he knew he was watched all the way to the door.

Standing on the corner, the traffic singing its aggressive

one-way song on his right, he looked left and saw, parked outside the grocer's shop, a white van, almost certainly the one he had seen as he danced in the gateway of the old Colville school.

Jonny already knew he was going back to Sophie's house, but it was not to be like the accidental, somehow ramshackle returns he had made previously, returns that were really failed departures. This one would be careful and deliberate, and this time he would stay until, finally, things were somehow achieved. He had set out looking for Bonny, but what he had found was Sophie, and in the last two days, without ever intending it, even after fighting against it, he had somehow assumed responsibility for her. Until that responsibility was passed on he could not walk away leaving her scrambling in her own dirt – possibly a prey to the same predators that had once preyed on him. He had to find some sort of evidence that her vulnerability was being exploited – something which he could take to some authority, and he had to arrange that she would be cared for. Jonny growled softly and complainingly to himself as he took out his wallet and counted his money. At last, irritated but determined, he went across the road to the post office and phoned his mother. The phone rang and rang. There was no answer.

After a little thought he spread the phone book open on the top of the coin box and began searching the yellow pages for an entry under *Old* hoping to find some reference to a place giving advice and support to people who had to look after elderly parents. But perhaps 'old' was a word that was too abrupt or tactless to use in the name of an institution. There was nothing between *Oil Refiners* and *Optical Instrument Servicing*. He tried to think of some other word for 'old' and after a moment looked under *Senior Citizens*, but all in vain. And the closest he could get to *Geriatric* was a list of geologists. After thinking again, he tried the main sequence in the phone book and did find an entry under *Senior Citizens*. However, it simply told him to refer to the name of the specific association, and gave no number at all. Try the hospital perhaps, Jonny thought, or the Red Cross, but then someone knocked on the glass door, tired of watching him occupying the box and doing nothing but turn pages. Jonny left the phone box and immediately began to think of other words meaning old... antique, ancient, out-of-date, last year's model, prehistoric, played-out, time out of mind...("Mind out of time," said Bonny in his head, her voice still working for him.)

Jonny withdrew more money, went back to the shopping centre, bought himself clean underpants, a comb, shaving foam and a razor, for he could see that it might be necessary to seem respectable some time in the very near future. With these purchases safely under his arm or in his pockets he went back to Sophie's house.

However, now he was obsessed with the idea that Nev

might be watching him from somewhere. The white van was still parked outside the shops, but Nev himself could be anywhere. Cruising around Colville was Nev's line, and all its hiding places would be known to him. Jonny wondered if Nev already knew where he was living. If so, he would guess that Jonny had recognised the radio, and if not, Jonny did not want him to find out. Moving in a great semicircle, like an animal disguising the track to its nest so that it could come and go undetected, Jonny followed the railway line, then picked his way through narrow, back streets in order to return safely to Sophie's house.

He arrived back at the green door at last and stood there, holding the key, looking up and down the one-way street. The only escape route from this city, this maze, lay, for him at least, beyond this door. Saturated as he was with memory, it seemed he must make his way home through a memory-desert which might drain some of the burden from him. Jonny grimaced scornfully at his own speculations.

"It isn't one of those great quests," he told the door, as he unlocked it at last and went in. On his third attempt at leaving he had got further than on any previous occasion, but in the end all paths led back to Sophie's house, which had not finished with him yet.

CHAPTER ELEVEN

Once more he climbed the stairs. The landing was the same but the cats were different, all smiling to see him returning, just as they had smiled to see him go.

"So *there* you are," Sophie said crossly as he came in at the door. "You're late, aren't you?"

Jonny sat down on the couch. Some cats had got so used to him they hardly shifted. One black-and-white cat turned over trustingly, revealing a soft, white stomach. Jonny stroked it obligingly while the cat kneaded the air, sensuously flexing claws like little flick knives. After a moment yet another cat tried to settle down on his knee.

"You just sit there," Sophie cried, "and I'll have something for you in a brace of shakes. A cup of tea is always most welcome."

"Tea and whatsitsnames," Jonny replied in the language of Sophie's house, although he already felt rather soggy with lemonade and beer. But making tea would keep her busy for a while.

Sophie vanished, and Jonny sat stroking the cat,

frowning thoughtfully. Although he did not know it, little by little his frown gave way to quite another expression. Little by little he began to smile rather sadly, and to shake his head over something, while out in the kitchen Sophie muttered and sighed, opening and shutting doors.

"So what's your advice?" he asked the cat which began to purr. "Really? You reckon?" Jonny looked astonished. "You wouldn't be prejudiced, would you?" The cat purred industriously. "What about Nev, though? Aha! You haven't got an answer to that, have you?" The cat, feeling some extra response was needed, butted his hand with its head. "I walked right into it," Jonny sighed. "Right now, I don't think I'll ever get away – unless they carry me out feet first."

After a while Jonny put the cat to one side. Things had to be done in the right order, and if he was to have a clean shirt for the following day, he would have to wash the one he had on. Down in the laundry he rinsed it, soaped it, rinsed it again, and put it in a bucket, thinking that if it was hung out wet, it might not need to be ironed. Then, having reduced, rather than removed the blood stains on his shirt, he sponged his blazer as well, carried shirt and blazer upstairs, and hung them both on the balcony line.

"That doesn't look too good," said Sophie, staring disapprovingly at his bare chest and shoulders.

"Actually most people think I'm pretty cool," Jonny told her.

"Well, I suppose you are. You're not wearing very much," she replied severely. Jonny laughed.

"OK – I'll put my hat on," he conceded, and did so, setting it at an angle, and moving over to the desk, where he stood staring at its pigeon-holes with resignation. In these little caves he might find, under the lavatory paper and banana skins, useful information for the proper authorities, something about Sophie and Errol, something about the house and the way the rent was paid. One pigeon-hole was now occupied by a grubby hairbrush. The one next to it held a tin lid full of dried cat food. The third held two pencils and a cake of soap. Into this magician's trick box things might vanish for ever, and other things might mysteriously appear. He opened a drawer imagining that it might reveal a void – planets, stars, a square of infinite night – but it was jammed with papers. Pulling up a chair he sat down at the desk and began taking things out, flicking lightly from one thing to another. There was plenty to puzzle over, though some things were straightforward enough. A Certificate of Entitlement had been issued by the Department of Social Welfare, proving that Sophie, being over sixty-five, received superannuation and was allowed to get into the cinema or travel on buses and planes at half price in between peak periods.

Then there was a stiff, folded piece of paper headed in official printing. It was a Register of Marriage issued in the city more than fifty years earlier. Sophia Elizabeth Carter had married Errol Matthew West at a registry office. She had been thirty-six years old when she married. Her mother's maiden name had been Rose Edith Babbitt. Jonny looked at this document with fascination, almost as if it marked the beginning of a new life, not only for Sophie and Errol in 1936 but, fifty years later, for Jonathan McKinley Dart, an honorary Babbitt.

"There's nothing to be ashamed of in being a Babbitt," he said to himself.

Sophie, carrying a teapot out to her little table, turned at his words.

"Well, they weren't from – how shall I put it – they weren't from the same class as the Carters," she said judicially, "but they were a good, hard-working family – except for Uncle Brian, that is, but he wasn't typical. I was very fond of your mother."

"And of me," said Jonny. Sophie gave a surprisingly wicked chuckle.

"Gosh, I don't know, Sophie," Jonny said, smiling back at her. "Sometimes I really worry about you!"

There were lots of pencils, and notebooks – some brand new – many reels of cotton, combs, a little pair of scissors, a teaspoon, a piece of apple – cored, peeled, brown and rotting on a willow-patterned saucer. Under all this Jonny found a whole series of post-office savings books, all in careful order, all annotated, all held together by a rubber band. There was nothing there after 1981.

"Where's the post-office savings book you use now?" Jonny asked Sophie as she set two cups on their saucers. "In your handbag, isn't it?"

"My handbag!" repeated Sophie doubtfully, as if she wasn't quite sure what a handbag was. Jonny sighed apprehensively, but then, glancing despairingly around the room, he saw a familiar red strap trailing out from under the couch like the lead of a dog.

When Sophie went out to the kitchen, he leaped triumphantly on the strap, the bag obediently came out of hiding, and he carried it back to the desk. Yet once there, the handbag squatting placidly on his knee, he grew unexpectedly shy, as if he were planning an intimate violation. He had searched the bag before, but always in Sophie's presence. This time he was taking it over. At last he opened it nervously and went though all its secret zippered pockets and little purses until he located not only the book he needed, but another one intended as a record for long-term deposits as well. There were very few entries in this second book. Jonny studied it while Sophie, flitting from kitchen to sitting room, set out yet another two cups on another two saucers.

"Gee!" Jonny exclaimed at last, rather impressed. Sophie looked up in surprise.

"You're quite rich, you know," he said wonderingly, shaking the book at her. "Do you know how much you've got saved up here?"

Sophie smiled sweetly at him, but her eyes were quite blank.

"I haven't gone without anything," she said, "but I've never run into debt. Errol always paid cash. 'If I pay cash will you give me discount?' That's what Errol used to say." She paused. "I think I sold the house," she added doubtfully. "Someone did."

Out in the kitchen the kettle screamed bad-temperedly.

"Oh, *there* it is," Sophie cried gladly and vanished.

Jonny's head rang like a till, metallic with money thoughts. He stared around the room in a much more speculative way than ever before, and found he could imagine himself living here very comfortably, slowly replacing Sophie's untidiness with his own. He could talk Sophie into buying a tape-deck – or even a whole stereo system. In return he could look after her, cook for her, have friends round after she was in bed... the fantasy ran on and on. A little earlier he had been furious at the thought that Nev might be exploiting her in some way, and now he was thinking about doing the same thing himself.

"You could be getting more interest for this, you know," he shouted in the direction of the kitchen. "You could afford a housekeeper, or a – a place that would look after you really well."

Sophie popped out of the kitchen. She was carrying a cup and a big enamel mug which she put on the table with the rest. "You need somebody to look after you," Jonny told her in a rather more subdued voice.

"I've got you," she pointed out with a loving smile.

"Yeah, well…" said Jonny heavily. "You need someone a lot better than me. You might need to be *protected* from me." He took up the savings book.

Sophie began to pour her tea. Jonny flicked from page to page. "I go funny at full moon," he said in a preoccupied voice, flattening the book open at one place and frowning over it. "You get superannuation automatically paid in," he said. "I can see the entries. That's straightforward."

Sophie sat looking down into her cup. She took no real interest at all in his efforts to understand her finances.

"Now, listen – listen, Sophie," Jonny insisted, pointing at the page. "Every month or so there's an automatic withdrawal of three hundred and twenty dollars – say, eighty dollars a week. Now, is that rent?"

Sophie peered at the spout of the teapot.

"This tea is very weak," she said in a puzzled voice.

"Sophie… you say you *think* you sold this house," Jonny persisted. "Do you pay rent?"

She continued to frown into one of the cups as if she were reading her fortune there.

"It's got Errol's name on the front," Jonny prompted her.

"Yes, but he's dead," she replied. "Didn't anyone tell you?"

"Do you pay rent?" Jonny cried despairingly, speaking as if she were deaf, pausing between each word for extra distinctness.

"I always get a receipt," she said brightly. "I've got a biscuit here for you... a plain biscuit. You don't have to worry about too much sugar in these biscuits. You know, I was reading somewhere only this morning that too much sugar and dairy produce is bad for you."

Jonny accepted a biscuit, and filed it away in a pigeon-hole with the cat food.

Tucked under the post-office savings books in their rubber band was a big manilla envelope, full of old photographs. Jonny spread them out and found he was looking at a younger Sophie: Sophie feeding ducks, Sophie standing at the back of the house by the tank-stand looking quizzically up at a huge sunflower which bent its face towards hers. There were scenes from some South Island holiday, photos that featured autumn colouring at Queenstown, and Sophie standing by an anonymous bridge, wonderful gold and scarlet trees behind her. She really did look like some sort of angel, surrounded by all that glow – though the scarlet leaves clashed rather badly with her crimson coat. There was a photograph of a middle-aged man sitting at a table in some garden tea-room, waving cheerfully at the camera. Jonny and Errol were face to face.

Sophie placed an enamel mug of warm water beside Jonny.

"You had an orange notebook when I first came here," he said. "You've hidden it somewhere. Do you know where it is?"

"I'll soon find it!" Sophie cried, her face lighting up with ambition.

She seized her handbag and began going through it while Jonny gloomily studied the next photograph: Errol standing on the balcony under the huge tap, looking somehow noble and patriotic as if plumbing were a great national principle like art or science. Now the drawer was empty – almost empty. As he restored the photographs, the corner of the envelope encountered a slight obstruction, and Jonny pulled out a thin, light, flat square wrapped in tissue paper... yet another photograph, kept apart from the others. The sepia image of a young man looked back at him, smiling, eyebrows raised, lips parted on the point of asking a question. He wore a striped blazer that might have been Jonny's own. Even without colour the resemblance was striking. So this was what Sophie saw with that faded, blue stare whenever she looked at him – not the man, but the blazer – the unforgettable blazer with its powerful stripes. Looking down at his sleeve, Jonny wondered if it could possibly be the same one. It was the sort of blazer that would never wear out... except for the elbows, of course. He turned the photo over and saw writing on the back: *Alva Babbitt 1926.*

"Are you the one?" Jonny said, nodding to Alva, but Alva kept his secrets. Over by the table Sophie sat staring hard at a dollar bill she had found in an obscure pocket of her handbag, frowning at it in a troubled way as if it were an important message in a secret code and she had lost the key. As Jonny watched, she put it down, took up a two-cent coin and began to study that instead. Jonny wrapped Alva in tissue paper again, and resumed his searching. After all, he had come back knowing it was going to be like this – boring, when it wasn't infuriating. Bonny wasn't going to knock on the door; Nev – even if Nev and Spike were the same person – wasn't going to appear suddenly like a special effect on television. The orange notebook full of addresses had vanished but, after all, this was Sophie's house. Perhaps the notebook had flashed out of existence for a while, and would flash back when it was ready, as the handbag had already done. He kept on searching, wandering into Sophie's bedroom and looking nervously at the closed drawers. Although he had searched them earlier in the day, by now they could be all changed around, holding either treasures or horrors. Sophie, prowling around her house continually, came up behind him.

"What are you doing here?" she asking, sounding puzzled. "I thought you were living in the North Island these days."

"I came to see you," Jonny explained. Sophie smiled knowingly at him. "Remember the old days?" he couldn't help saying, and a great softness spread over her face.

"It was out of the question – us being cousins," she said. Jonny thought of Alva wrapped in tissue paper, pushed to the back of the drawer.

"Oh, I don't know," he said at last. "It's legal for cousins to marry, and mostly their kids are all right."

"My father thought it was best avoided," Sophie said firmly. "He was an MA, you know – a very clever man."

"Oh, well, we can still be good friends, can't we?" said Jonny. "If Errol comes home unexpectedly I'll hide in the wardrobe."

"You will not," said Sophie outraged. "You can just run out the back..."

"...like an honest man," Jonny finished.

"Yes," Sophie agreed. "I would never ever be mixed up in anything that wasn't honest. I would never, never do anything dishonest. I always pay promptly and I always get a receipt. I never owe anything." She paused. "You never ever got to know Errol, did you?"

"I heard he was one of nature's gentlemen," Jonny said. Sophie beamed at him.

"You've taken the very words from out of my mouth," she said. "That's just what *I* was going to say. Now, how about a cup of tea?"

"Great!" said Jonny.

A moment later he heard her rattling things in the cupboards, and remembered a small bundle of papers tucked into a crimson glove, secured with a rubber band, somewhere in a kitchen drawer. It had probably been tidied away somewhere else, he thought, going in search of it, but there it was, just where he had left it the day before. Carrying it back to the desk, he began to sort through its contents, although he had given up expecting to find anything that would cast any certain light upon Sophie's rent, or the identity of Spike, the landlord, who just might be Nev Fowler.

The first envelope he took from the glove was a long manilla envelope which had never been opened. He read the address: *Miss B. Benedicta, 115 Marribel Road.*

Jonny sat and stared, then he stood up slowly. This time he would get it right. First he checked his pocket for the key, and then went out on to the balcony to inspect his washing. The shirt was still soaking wet, of course, but the blazer, though damp in patches, was wearable. Frightened of moving too precipitately, of jolting accident and changing the pattern, he moved softly upstairs on tiptoe and collected *A History of Angels,* lying open beside his bed.

A moment later he was out in the street, looking at the number on Sophie's door. '113' it said very clearly. He looked at the next-door house, moving over to study its door. There was nothing to be seen on the balcony. The door was firmly shut. '115' said the number, painted on in neat, black letters. Jonny looked from the door to the letter in his hand, and then back to the door again. Then he knocked and listened. After a while he knocked once more. As he knocked the second time, he heard quick footsteps coming downstairs towards the door. They came very quickly. He barely had time to finish knocking before the door opened.

Bonny Benedicta stood before him. He recognised her at once, beyond any doubt, though she was entirely different from the way he had remembered her, neat and plain in ordinary tight blue jeans and a floppy grey sweater.

"Hello," said Jonny foolishly. "Remember me?" She had been staring at him quite expressionlessly, but as he spoke, she began to smile, and then to laugh.

"Jonny Dart," she said to him. "You've been looking for me. What's taken you so long?"

CHAPTER TWELVE

Jonny stood with the letter and the book held out like offerings, unable to believe what he was seeing. For years Janine and Bonny, light and dark, had towered over him like goddesses. They had invented a world for him and had moved him around it, forecasting his future and telling him what to do.

Now, he was astounded to find Bonny – who had stood so tall in his memory – slight, even delicate. The starry clothes, the glittering chains at throat and wrist were gone; she was not wearing a single ring. Her long, tangled hair still scribbled down over her shoulders like the hair of the past Bonny but, though her skin was indeed the colour of bush-honey, there was cinnamon and ginger mixed in it too. He had remembered her cool and plain, and here she was not only warm but camouflaged with large, light freckles. It was Bonny's shadow he had seen moving on the brick wall, her duplicate which had held out its hands to him from the balcony. Though he had not recognised her until now, they had been living side by side in the stop and start of the city's jungle. But was Bonny still a Pythoness? She was not tall, not cool, not shadowy. Her smile was not mysterious. It was almost jolly.

"Were you expecting me?" he stammered, copying her smile as if he were her mirror. "How?"

"My mother *warned* me that you were on my trail," Bonny cried. Jonny recovered quickly.

"I'll bet," he said shortly.

"How did you find me?" Bonny asked him. "I'm on the phone, but not in the book." Even her voice was not as he had remembered it. It was still deep, but not musical. It was rather croaky – comical, not beautiful.

She began explaining something, waving her lively ringless hands, but an articulated truck rolled by behind them, the air filling with diesel fumes. Bonny's warm lips smiled and moved, but her words were sucked into the vacuum which the truck made around itself, and they both automatically hunched their shoulders as the passing storm swept by, simply staring at one another, waiting for it to end.

Then Bonny took him by the wrist and drew him into her house, shutting the door behind him. Once again Jonny stood in a dim hall at the foot of a dog-leg stair. There was no supermarket trolley full of shoes; there were no cats. He couldn't help believing that this was the place he had meant to arrive at but that there had been another computer fault in destiny, and he had wound up in Sophie's house instead – a near miss!

"How did you find me?" Bonnie demanded, her fingers clasped over his wrist rather as if she planned to read the truth of his answer from his heart-beat.

"I was guided," he answered.

"How?" she asked.

"It was written on me." Jonny looked blankly into his left palm. "I woke up on the island. I set off walking in this direction, and that's how I came to meet Sophie. Then there was the street name – Marribel Road. I knew it meant something. I must have remembered it without ever knowing I was remembering," he cried incredulously, "and so in the end I went home with Sophie."

But Bonny had no idea what he was talking about. He was more fantastic than familiar.

"Sophie West, next door," Jonny explained and, once again, held out the book and the envelope as mute evidence. Bonny at last understood they were intended for her, took them, looked at him as if he were playing a trick on her, then opened the book, read her name in it, and laughed, as if he had asked her a riddle she couldn't answer. But Jonny did not know the answer either.

"Where on earth did you get this?" she cried.

"Sophie brought it in, like dogs bring things," Jonny explained. "She told me a man had given it to her – someone in pink or yellow. But that doesn't necessarily mean anything. She asked me what I made of it."

"Are you actually living with that little old lady who

steals my milk bottles?" Bonny asked. It was her turn to be incredulous.

"If you can call it living," Jonny said doubtfully. "We make it all up as we go along."

"Oh, well – that's living, all right." Bonny relaxed, sounding amused once more. "I can recognise that. My mother made you sound as if you'd been freshly killed, but she was exaggerating as usual."

"Not by much!" Jonny said seriously. "I've improved a lot since Monday."

In the beginning, Bonny had had to pause and think before recognising him. Now that she knew who he was she had begun noticing details – his bare chest under the striped blazer, the angle of his bandit hat, the mottled bracket that took one of his eyes out of context with the rest of his face.

"Goodness – what on earth has happened to the neat, little, kind boy I've been remembering all this time?" she asked lightly. Jonny considered this description.

"You left out 'handsome'!" he pointed out.

"Now, that's not just fishing for a compliment, that's forcing one." Bonny smiled faintly – almost a Pythoness smile. "Just tell me what happened to him – to you."

Jonny felt his own expression alter, as he looked up into the air over her head.

"That dear little boy didn't make it," he told her. "Poor little chap – he split open one day, and *I* came out. I'd been growing inside him all the time – like in a horror film."

"Jonny! Terrific!" Bonny said, clapping softly and ironically in the shadow of the stair. Jonny grinned sheepishly, though he had told nothing but the truth.

"Do you want me to tell you all about it standing around down here?" Jonny asked. "Ask me in properly. Be polite."

Bonny hesitated. In the beginning she had been not only surprised to see him, but pleased, too… Jonny was sure she had been pleased. Yet now he could see she was wondering whether or not to invite him up her staircase.

"It's actually an awkward day for me to have a visitor," she explained. "I've got a deadline – work I have to give to my tutor tomorrow. I can't afford a social life."

"You won't have to feed me or anything," he promised rather stiffly.

Bonny shook her head as if she were disagreeing with him, but then said, "Oh, why not?" mostly to herself, and led the way up the crooked stair. On the landing Jonny glanced upwards towards the door which, in Sophie's house, was the door of his bedroom. He wondered if Bonny slept behind the same door. He thought she probably did and, if she did, it was almost as if they had been sharing the same bed, made invisible to each other by a spell, now broken. Turning restlessly in secret, separate nights, they had come face to face at last, just as they *had* to, as he and Nev had already done. The funny thing was that Nev and he had known each other at once, but finding Bonny was like finding a stranger... though a stranger with occasional disconcerting resemblances to an old friend.

Following her obediently through the sitting room door, he came into a room without a desk or a table, or a tartan settee – a room with its windows open wide. From the rough, brownish-green lawn, an old, revolving clothesline, lying on its side, faced them like the dish of a radio telescope waiting to catch every significant thing they were about to say. Grass grew tall along the wall on which, only two nights ago, shadows had twitched and argued. It was not much of a view, but the real views of this house were all inwards. Jonny, no great reader himself, was impressed with its wild geography. Bookcases, improvised from bricks and boards, climbed up the wall, but all the shelves were overflowing, and books sprawled out from them, escaping in all directions. Between the shelves, columns of books, piled one on top of another, rose towards the ceiling, stalagmites of pages, word laid down on word, whole stratas of ideas.

Jonny and Bonny turned to face each other like antagonists, held apart by silence. The further he came into her house, the more she defended herself against him for, of her two great adventures, she had kept only one. She was still older than he was, and was still entitled to look at him in the way a kindly, older person looks at a younger one. But now she had to direct this gaze upwards, for he was much the taller. Though height was an unintentional victory, it was as if he had conquered part of Bonny for ever.

The silence persisted, and Jonny looked around desperately for something to talk about. There were many subjects, but it was hard to begin a conversation with any of them. And in an odd way they seemed to have company. Standing beside the door to the kitchen was the faceless woman of the balcony, now wearing a wig of romantic black curls and a straw sun hat, its brim weighed down with charms and earrings and artificial flowers. Not only that, she was dressed for an amazing party, hung with layers of clothes in bright colours, many of them painted, or illustrated in some way, with pictures, signs, emblems, or printed with the beginning and endings of words which had to be guessed at. Around its neck dangled chains, ribbons, pendants. The shirt on the top was not only painted with a sun on one breast and a moon on the other, but was pinned over with brooches, clips and badges of many kinds. Though she had no face, Jonny recognised her more than he had recognised Bonny. Here, among grottos and towers and bridges of books, was the Pythoness, run to ground at last, faceless and therefore enigmatic. Jonny was able to fill in from memory or imagination – by now it didn't matter which – a closed smile, and oblique Chinese eyes. At the open window stood an old, clumsy oak table, papers and pens spread across it, a little typewriter squatting comfortably among them.

"This book – I loaned it to a friend," Bonny explained at last, shaking the book a little reprovingly at Jonny. "Your Sophie must have seen him drop it off again in my letterbox and stolen it. She's a problem as a neighbour."

"And as a hostess," Jonny said, grinning. (*My* Sophie? he was thinking, horrified. Mine!) "She invited me in, but now I can't get away, and I have to do all the cooking."

"She specialises in stealing milk and letters," Bonny explained. "If there's nothing in her box she comes over to mine. I tried putting a padlock on it but then she set to with a little chopper and chopped her way in."

Jonny found it easy to imagine Sophie, cross and dogged, striking at Bonny's letterbox in the same fierce way she had struck at the wall-socket with the plug of the toaster, getting nasty with a world that had suddenly turned on her and shut her out of its secrets.

"Not that I get much mail," Bonny went on, "but all the same..." Jonny looked guilty on Sophie's behalf. "I *did* think about shifting, but in the end I got a post-office box instead. I'm so weighed down." She gestured at the books around her. "And besides, it's really cheap to live here. They don't do any maintenance because it's scheduled for demolition within a year."

"Why?" asked Jonny, looking around the room. Although it was not fashionable or beautiful, it appeared to be sturdy enough. There were no leaks that he could see. He had noticed none in Sophie's house.

"Oh, it belongs to some group of accountants who own quite a bit of land around here. They're waiting for the lease to run out on the car park," Bonny explained. "Then they'll put up some big development... I don't know what."

Jonny, who had been listening to Bonny, but looking at the faceless Pythoness, felt a peculiar thrill as he recognised a clue to something in the life next door. He stared at her very hard.

"Who do you pay the rent to?" he demanded sharply. Taken aback by his tone, she paused, lips parted, straight, dark eyebrows slightly raised.

"A firm of accountants," she replied. "Probably the owners. Why?" ("What business is it of yours?" she was really asking him.)

"Someone's ripping Sophie off," he explained. "I think I know who it is, too, but there's no proof."

"You must have some reason for thinking so," Bonny said, sounding inquisitive, but Jonny could not be bothered explaining about the pink receipts.

"I feel it *here*," he replied, placing his hands on his heart, smiling as he did so. "If I catch him at it, I'll really sort him out... sort him to bits." And then, hearing how sincere he sounded, he said quickly, "Am I allowed to sit down?"

Bonny looked around vaguely.

"You're allowed to sit where you can," she told him.

"There must be a place. I've got a beanbag, and there's my typing chair – oh, and some floor cushions." There was detachment rather than real hospitality in her voice. But then she added, "I'm just a little bit taken aback by all this... One moment I'm thinking hard about the nature of metaphor, and then suddenly, a hand that reaches from the past comes knocking on my door at last."

She was making fun of the past, but at her words the five years since their last strange hour together shrank away to nothing, and the old Bonny and the present one ran together like two colours. After all, his very first thoughts of love had been about Bonny Benedicta and, once upon a time, she had put her arms around him as they stood overlooking the space that had swallowed his sister. For Jonny, standing in the cave of books, it was as if he and Bonny had trembled and wept and clung to one another on the edge of the cliff only a few seconds earlier. This was the point from which their conversation should begin, from the point where those opposites, love and death, had rushed together in his blood, as past and present did now. But he understood all this in signs which, not being words, couldn't be used to explain anything.

"How are your parents?" he asked, for something to say.

"You've seen them more recently than I have," Bonny replied, amused by him yet again. "How did they seem?"

"Fine," Jonny had to admit. "They were throwing a party." Silence tried to come between them once more. "Who

176

was the bloke you were arguing with in the early hours of... of Tuesday, it must have been?" he asked suddenly, amazed at his own question, which had seemed to ask itself.

"Never you mind who it was," Bonny said guardedly. "Just tell me how *your* parents are instead."

"Fine, when I saw them last," Jonny sighed. "Was he a boyfriend?"

"He's a grown man, but that's my business," Bonny retorted, obviously irritated, but laughing in spite of it.

"I'm just taking an interest, making conversation," Jonny explained. "I didn't hear anything you were saying. I just watched your shadows for about ten seconds."

"What are you doing with yourself, anyway?" Bonny asked, firmly distracting him, dragging a beanbag cushion towards him. Jonny had a rhyme of his own – one he had worked out for himself at the beginning of the year.

"Out of work – on the dole, in flames and out of control," he answered, clapping soundlessly, dancing eight measures on the spot, turning in a circle on his left foot while marking in the taps with the right. "The trouble is it sounds wishy-washy in sneakers," he added deprecatingly. "And it needs the right backing to be a real hit. I have applied for jobs but, so far, no luck."

"Ah, yes – but why aren't you something big in the entertainment world by now?" Bonny asked him, a little mockingly. She had never seemed impressed by the temporary fame that had once surrounded Jonny and Janine.

"You know why, you were there," Jonny said. He dropped down into the beanbag, surrendering the advantage of height quite readily. "The star of the show took off, didn't she?"

He waited a little tensely for her to say something, thinking they were once more approaching the great topic that lay uneasily between them. Like pirates in an adventure story dividing a significant gold coin or a treasure map, they had half a memory each, but because of shyness or because five years had passed, Jonny saw they might never match the two halves up again. When Bonny didn't reply, he sighed and shrugged. "I'm a man with a great future behind me."

"Fishing for compliments again," Bonny said scornfully. "You were the true dancer. Everyone knew that, even Janine."

Jonny was too astounded to reply at once.

"Who ever told you that? I'll bet Janine didn't," he said at last, disbelievingly.

"As it happens, she did." Bonny had her back to him, pulling a large floor cushion free from books and papers. "Janine always told the truth, even if she didn't like it. And I was always prepared to listen to it – to her particular version of it, anyway. That's what brought us together. It doesn't happen often – a combination like that – once in a thousand years, say."

She picked up the cushion and thumped it hard. "But

she didn't have to tell me about you. Anyone could see it... well, not all the time, of course – just every now and then. So we were both jealous of you! What was it you said you wanted? Tea?"

"No, thanks," Jonny said quickly. "Not really." He was greedy to be told more. "Listen, Janine was the one who always sold us at auditions."

"Oh, Janine was a real entertainer," Bonny said. "She made everything look good, but you were the real dancer. I used to think you had some sort of a secret agreement with space."

Well, there you are, Jonny thought. Even small, and freckled and croaky, even in plain clothes, she brings off revelations. Once a Pythoness always a Pythoness. Of course Bonny might be making fun of him, but she sounded too matter-of-fact for that. Besides, what she was saying matched up with something he had often felt about his own dancing. Although he had enjoyed being on stage, had enjoyed making the television ads, he had never felt transformed by public occasions, whereas private dancing had been another matter. Sometimes, just practising, hearing the intricate and inevitable pattern his feet were inscribing on the earth, he had believed he was really drawing it up *out* of the heart of things, and had felt remarkable.

"It's a very abstract talent," Bonny said, as if she were reading his thoughts and finishing them off for him.

Though she had found a cushion for herself Bonny had so far refused to commit herself to sustained conversation by sitting on it. Instead, she stood in front of him, hugging the cushion as if she couldn't quite make up her mind what to do next. Jonny couldn't make up his mind either. He was feeling very urgent about something, but the urgency refused to form itself into proper questions. In most ways they didn't know one another well enough to gossip or confide, but had once shared too much to talk easily about trivial things now. All the same, he had to say something, or offer to go home.

"What about *your* sister?" he asked. "I didn't see her the other night. Is she still living at home?"

Bonny's eyes shifted a little. It was her turn to look into space.

"These sisters..." she said at last. "We could probably spend a whole afternoon talking about sisters and what they get up to." And then she looked towards the table as if she were longing for him to leave so that she could get back to her books. Jonny did not budge.

"So?" he asked. "Is she?"

"Is she what?"

"Is she living at home doing organic farming and recycling things?"

"She's been too busy for anything like that," Bonny said shortly. "She's got no time for all that middle-class *pakeha**

* A New Zealander of predominantly European cultural identity.

academic scene. She's involved with a central city women's collective, with an emphasis on Polynesian affairs, and she does work for the *kohanga reo* movement, and she teaches traditional Maori crafts... She's changed her names." Bonny frowned as if she were giving the information against her will.

"Names? You only change one when you get married," Jonny said, quoting an authority.

"No – she changed it by deed poll. She tracked down her natural mother, and took on her name – Hotene."

Jonny was astounded.

"Hotene! Not Hinerangi Hotene, the beautiful activist?" he asked, but he already knew what the answer must be. Bonny nodded. "Hinerangi Hotene – the one that threw an explosive device at the Minister of Maori Affairs? *Samantha?*"

"That very one," Bonny answered.

"Gosh," said Jonny feebly. "All those lessons in ballet and reading *Winnie-the-Pooh* and she's gone back to the *marae.** All that culture for nothing."

Bonny's straight, strong eyebrows drew in across her nose, her mouth tightened, her yellow-brown eyes looked over the cushion like an eagle's eyes.

"She's got a true cause," she said in a flat, bored voice, though Jonny quickly understood she was not bored but

* Marae: a space in front of a Maori meeting house, often used for community social life and hospitality.

very angry. "She follows it with all her heart. She knows just who she is. Don't be so – so plastic."

"OK," said Jonny amicably. "I am a bit plastic. You be all wholesome and biodegradable and I'll be plastic, and we'll see who rots down first." Bonny's sombre expression grew lighter and more entertained.

"Fight against it," was all she said.

Jonny wanted to know more. Torn with curiosity, he couldn't help wondering just what the Drs Benedicta thought about their younger daughter getting the style and advantages of her respectable adoptive name and then giving it up. And was Bonny also ambitious to follow the streams of her mixed blood to their sources? However, he hesitated, feeling there was something difficult in the subject, and it seemed that they might be about to suffer yet another silence, and this time he would have to say it was nice to have met her again – and then go.

"ONCE IN THE OLD DAYS," sang the band in his head, and Jonny leaped up, looking beyond Bonny to the model in its layers of painted clothes.

"Let me tell you a story..." he said to it, taking the cool hand at the end of its outstretched arm and propping the other over his shoulder. Then he lifted it, stand and all, and, clasping it to him, looked tenderly into its blank face. It was quite heavy, yet not so much heavy as clumsy. All the same, he began to dance with it. "You look very charming tonight," he said to it. "You are so mysterious, such a true

Pythoness. Be mine!" He swept it past Bonny. "This is a tango!" he told her over its shoulder. As he and the dummy circled her, Bonny turned her head, following them.

"What's that?" Jonny asked the dummy. "You have a dark past? So have I! You show me yours and I'll show you mine." And he began to tell it his story, every now and then nodding solemnly at Bonny over its shoulder. "I woke up on the island," he began. "There was no ocean. All around me the city was silent and full of shadows. I began to *go go, go to gone gone gone.*" It was so much easier for him to tell a story when he was partly dancing it. "But who is this coming across the stone desert to meet me?" he asked dramatically.

Revolving slowly, then reversing in the tiny compass of the cave of books, he told of meeting Sophie, of taking her shopping, of giving her a bath. The model slipped sideways in his arms, jingling faintly. He told of his three attempts to escape from Sophie's house, of his encounter with Nev, his return, and the discovery of Bonny's address on the letter. As he danced with his inert partner he found himself increasingly impressed with the way he had earned, through a sort of fidelity to chance, the gift of a slow revelation.

"So I walked up the stairs," he said to the dummy, "and there you were, the Pythoness, wearing Pythoness clothes." Coming to a standstill, he said to Bonny, "I've always imagined you wearing them, but you look very straight these days."

"Eccentric clothes are too easy," Bonny replied. "You come to depend on them too much. Jonny, it's typical of me, though," she said rather bitterly as he put the dummy down, spinning it lightly on its stand. "I've lived next to Mrs West for over a year now and I've never once done one thing to help her. I've never really noticed she was so... so..."

"...far out?" Jonny suggested. "But I took over from someone already set up in her head – a cousin she was keen on. I think he used to wear a blazer like mine. She can talk about the weather and sound quite reasonable – well, fairly reasonable."

"But most people would have *just walked on by* and left her," Bonny said, singing back to him, as he had sung to her. "Jonny Dart, you haven't changed so much, after all."

Jonny did not bother to reply but simply tapped his discoloured cheek. "Oh, I know all about that..." she cried. "But when you were little you were always bringing hurt birds home, trying to keep them warm and giving them crumbs. You were always kind."

"They always died," Jonny replied after a pause. "It wasn't really worth it."

His past compassion for weak things was something he very seldom remembered about himself.

"You used to get very upset when they died," Bonny recalled. "You cared about them *passionately*."

"I only made them suffer more," he said at last. "A really kind person would have put them out of their misery."

"I don't think you could choose," Bonny said. "Not really. It's part of the way you are. And I'm always off to one side, missing what's right in front of me – maybe avoiding it. That's the way I am."

"Anyone could have lived next to Sophie without really knowing," Jonny said, dimly feeling that, for all her dry tone, Bonny was blaming herself for something. "I mean – she goes backwards and forwards in her hat and coat, just stealing the odd milk bottle. Nobody knows the worst until they've seen the state of her ironing board." He hurried on quickly. "Hey, listen, though! Perhaps you could tell me. Isn't there somewhere where an old person who's lost her memory and doesn't cook for herself, and doesn't ever wash, can get help?"

"She'd need to go into a home of some kind," Bonny said. "You'd need to ask her family."

"I don't know if she has any family," Jonny explained. "Errol was one of nature's gentlemen and they didn't have any kids. Anyhow, he's dead. There's only me, and she thinks I'm someone else. What she needs is someone to come and look at her, and give approval for her to get meals-on-wheels or a district nurse or something like that."

He had the feeling that Bonny was bothered by what he had just said, but when she answered, her voice was quite bright, even triumphant.

"I know – the Aged People's Welfare Council! A friend of my mother's works there. Go and ask for Mr Dainton."

"*Aged!*" Jonny exclaimed. "Wouldn't it rock you? I tried 'old', I tried 'senior', I think I even tried 'ancient'!"

"I'll draw you a map," Bonny said, sounding pleased because she had thought of something useful to do. Picking up a pen from the table she began to draw busily. "It's not hard to find."

Sharing concern for Sophie was something they could be at one over for a little while, Jonny thought, but then, as Bonny finished the drawing, she looked at the books and papers spread over the table.

"Jonny," she said. "I really was working when you knocked on the door. I do have stuff to get in to my tutor tomorrow. I'm going to have to throw you out now because I must get it done."

"I'll go quietly," Jonny replied, hiding his frustration that they had met and talked so much, and yet had said so little. And now Bonny seemed to be waiting for him to say something else, and he couldn't think what it might be.

"At least I know where you are," he remarked, taking the map from her.

"Aren't you going to tell me?" she asked.

"Tell you what?"

"Tell me why you were looking for me? Why you went to visit my parents at midnight, and why you followed Mrs West down Marribel Road? Was it just for a bit of gossip about old times?"

"No," said Jonny. "Well, not exactly."

"Tell me, then."

"Its sense has gone." As they stood in the cave of books facing each other they were both perplexed at being so close and yet not connecting.

"My mother said you were bringing me something," Bonny said. A tide of colour crept into Jonny's face.

"Oh, that!" he said. "It's just a thing I've carried around with me for years, and it suddenly came to me that I might give it back to you. But I was drunk. She probably told you."

Bonny was intrigued.

"I've been looking forward to a present," she said, so Jonny put his hand into the top pocket of his blazer and brought out something he had found after days of searching in the meadow grasses of the reserve, a golden serpent with its tail in its own mouth. But when Bonny saw it, she stepped back, staring at it in horror.

"I threw it away," she cried. "I remember throwing it away."

"I found it again," Jonny explained. "I didn't get a chance to give it back to you at the funeral."

"Jonny, truly, I don't want it," Bonny declared. "That's all over and done with."

"The good old days." Jonny took the hand of the model. "Be mine!" he said to it, and slid the ring on to its finger. "I'm betrothed to the Pythoness. It's an engagement of long standing – anyway she can't sit down. I can see myself out. I know the way."

Bonny had watched him put the ring on the cold hand very apprehensively. Suddenly, she laughed.

"I don't know what's wrong with me!" she said, as they went down the stairs together. "I'll pass my work in tomorrow and I'll be taking a break tomorrow night, so why don't you bring Mrs West over for dinner... a neighbourly party," she added.

Jonny was flooded with relief. He felt as if he had been given a second chance, without quite knowing what the second chance was for.

"Better still, I'll invite *you*," he said. "I can only cook one thing, but I can cook it quite well. I've visited you. Now, it's your turn to visit me – me and Sophie."

In the doorway, the roaring street only a step away, Bonny allowed herself to ask about his bruises.

"I must say it does look as if someone has been trying to kill you," she remarked. Jonny laughed.

"Oh, that! That's just a bit of – you know – gratuitous violence," he said cheerfully.

"Like in the good old days?" she asked. Jonny, out on the street, turned to face her again.

"Almost, but not quite," he answered. "I was the one who started it this time. Why wait for it to come to you?"

"You used to be so submissive," Bonny said with a sigh. Jonny considered this.

"I was taught to submit," he said at last, "but now I've *un*learned it. Samantha – beg your pardon, Hinerangi – is being a self-taught Maori, and I'm self-taught, too."

"She feels it passionately," exclaimed Bonny. "It's part of her."

"This is part of me," said Jonny touching his face.

He was startled to see how dark it was outside. Twilight had fallen over the city while he sat in Bonny's house. Only now, on the threshold, did he come close to talking about the things that had brought him there in the first place.

"Hey, Bonny! Do you ever think about – about Janine, falling like that?"

He could scarcely see her face. The light was behind her.

"I think of it every day," she answered. "Goodnight, Jonny."

Jonny walked several paces up the one-way street, opening Sophie's door with Sophie's key. Immediately he noticed a new smell in the overloaded air. Upstairs something was burning. He bounded frantically upwards, through the sitting room and into the empty kitchen.

CHAPTER THIRTEEN

The stove was turned on. The ring was red hot. The frying pan in which he had poached eggs earlier was sitting on the ring with a cheerful fire blazing in it while a cloud of black smoke rose from the flames to hover about the ceiling. Sophie had apparently decided to melt butter. It looked like a small but effective atomic explosion.

"Is that you, Errol?" Sophie called from the bedroom.

"Near enough!" Jonny shouted back. "Anyhow, you won't do any better these days." He seized the handle of the frying pan as he shouted, searing his fingers. He dropped it, swearing. Sophie came out and looked at him sternly.

"Please don't throw my crockery around," she said haughtily, quite ignoring the flames leaping up from the floor.

"Watch out! Watch out!" Jonny yelled, making a glove out of a tea-towel, scooping the pan up and dropping it in the sink. Sophie watched him disapprovingly.

"You should be more careful," she told him crossly. "Where have you been? I was waiting for you."

"I've only been next door," said Jonny. However, he felt that he had been much further. Only a few metres away, through walls that felt frail as tissue, Bonny would be moving around her cave of books, and although their meeting had been bewildering and unsatisfactory, his mind was already active with cleverer things he might have said which might have commanded her attention and made everything turn out differently. Of course, he could always go back and work them into the conversation somehow but, on the whole, it might be better to wait for the following evening. It would give him time to practise.

"How about sausages for dinner?" he asked Sophie. She frowned and pursed her lips.

"Oh, I don't know about that," she replied gravely, "because sausages can be rather fatty, you know, and I was reading somewhere that too much fat isn't good for you."

"I'll cook them in some non-fatty way," lied Jonny, and her face grew sunny once more.

"Oh, that's all right then," she said, "because I think you've got to be careful about fats. No fats, no white sugar. Now, Errol used to take sugar in his tea, and I often think he would have been better without it, but menfolk like sweet things."

"That's why I'm so fond of you, Sophie," Jonny said daringly.

"That's enough of that!" she cried sternly, and then spoiled it by giggling. "Oh dear, oh dear, oh dear!"

Sausages are supposed to be easy to cook, but in the past when he had been a Boy Scout, Jonny had had a lot of trouble with them. This time, determined to get things right, he boiled them cautiously for a few minutes then, draining the water away, replaced it with a lump of butter, and fried them in the saucepan, for the frying pan was now impossible to use. Then he drenched them with tomato sauce. Sophie ate hers greedily and mopped up the sauce with a slice of bread.

They did the dishes companionably, and settled down to watch the animated film of *Watership Down* on television. Jonny studied the screen with the intense stare of someone who knows that nothing better is available, and tried not to think of Bonny bent over her typewriter, though perhaps that story about needing to work had been an excuse to get rid of him. He wondered about the early-morning argument he had almost overhead and wished he had listened in on it. Had the shadows been cast from Bonny's sitting room or from her bedroom? He sighed uneasily. In the part of the imagination that hides itself from common sense he had come to believe that he and Bonny were somehow not exactly in love but promised to each other. He had invested the memory of their embrace by the danger-sign with a significance so secret he was only just aware of it himself. He had turned up on Bonny's doorstep unshaven, battered under the bandit hat, half-naked under his blazer and had somehow believed she would want him.

"It's amazing what they can teach rabbits to do these days," Sophie exclaimed suddenly. "Even talking!"

Jonny remembered that once, when he was small, he had wept so loudly at seeing some cartoon cat run over by a truck, then crushed between the cymbals of a street band, that his father had had to carry him screaming from the theatre. Once upon a time he, too, had been taken in by active, talking shadows, just as Sophie was now.

"These rabbits... they're looking for a home, Sophie," he explained.

"Well, I can understand that," Sophie said tolerantly. "You know, I think a woman needs a home of her own. It's not the same living with your mother. Errol and I were very happy in this house after a while. His father built it, you know, this one and the house next door, and he used the best timber and the best nails. Errol used to say, 'This house will be here in a hundred years.'"

Jonny looked around at the sturdy walls, at the ceiling with its countless banners of grey lace, knowing uneasily that the wild city was lapping at the door, and that bulldozers and other demolition machines were slowly closing in.

"It'll stand for ever, this house," said Sophie comfortably.

"Wouldn't you like somewhere different?" Jonny asked. "Smaller? Somewhere with no stairs?"

"Well..." Sophie considered this carefully. "It might be

convenient, but I'm used to the dear old place. I know where everything goes."

Stunted figures – foreshortened rabbits – leaped across the screen; voices cried and sang. Sophie laid her arms along the arms of her chair. Her head bobbed down, her shoulders bent forward.

"It's nice to be with someone of your own," she murmured sleepily.

I've really left home, Jonny thought with amazement. How did that happen? Even when he arrived back at his family house tomorrow – or the next day – things would not be the same, for he would have done what his father had declared he could never do: he would have managed on his own, and they would have managed without him. Whatever gap he had left behind him would already be slowly closing up. Of course, his father would be bewildered and not entirely pleased to see him now, sitting in such peculiar company. He had wanted the sort of son who would run away to sea or build a business empire rather than one who fried sausages for old ladies. It was not what Jonny would have planned, either. Sophie nodded and drowsed, and Jonny thought of Bonny yet again, wondering why he bothered, when he was more comfortable sitting here with Sophie than he had been in Bonny's company. Still, he began going back over the good old days, fitting the new Bonny into the spaces the vanishing Pythoness left behind... a little girl with freckles trying to give herself a rare, exotic shape by painting clothes and playing with cards.

Sophie slumped forward. Jonny seized her, terrified that she would bang her head on the wooden arm of the chair. She was not hurt, though she easily could have been, but his hand on her arm frightened her.

"Now then, no need for that," she cried huffily, and Jonny released her quickly.

"You'd better go to bed," he told her. "It's late, Sophie. You were asleep in your chair."

"Oh dear, oh dear," she said getting to her feet, and stretching rather prettily, Jonny thought, not unlike a little cat herself. "Yes! Bed will be most acceptable. I'll make a cup of tea."

"We've only just had one," Jonny lied quickly, thinking of wet mattresses. "I don't think it would be a good idea to have another."

"I'll have to straighten things up," Sophie declared and began going backwards and forwards very busily, like a clockwork woman wound up to go, picking things up, staring at them, folding them, putting them away, taking them out, shaking them, folding them again, thumping the cushions quite brutally, and putting them on other chairs in a different order. Jonny could see that she was longing to be busy and useful, but wasn't able to organise her energy properly. Taking off her shoes she put one of them into the pigeon-hole of her desk. After staring at it keenly for a little while she sighed deeply and took it out again, putting both shoes on top of the desk, and vanished at last. Jonny heard her bed complaining a little as she got into it. For himself, he went on watching television, hoping when the news came on for any picture of Hinerangi Hotene, but she was not mentioned tonight. Already the Land Marches were old history. After a while he went to sleep in his chair, just as Sophie had done.

Somewhere in his sleep he heard Sophie's bed creak again, but it did not wake him. Perhaps he was dreaming; certainly his sleep seemed to be full of voices. "You'll be back!" his father shouted. "Smile!" cried his mother. "You'll never catch up with me!" Janine declared scornfully, moving just ahead of him along the ridge. If he put his hand out he could have touched her. If he had put his hand out he could have... "It'll make a man of you," promised Nev. "FROM BIG MOTHER DARKNESS NAKED WE COME," his favourite band sang in his ear. Sleep had become his Walkman. "BIG BROTHER FEAR'S GOT EVERYONE'S NAME ON FILE. SO SMILE!" they sang, and Jonny opened his eyes.

Sophie was standing directly in front of him. She was quite naked. Her eyes were round but she was seeing him.

"Alva," she said in a slow, sighing voice that he had never heard her use before. She was holding something in one hand but she laid the other hand, her left one, against his cheek. "It breaks my heart," she said, and her voice was still old but not cosy. It was ragged with despair. "I'll never get over it," she told him. "I'll never love anyone else, never, never, never."

Jonny sat up very slowly. He stared straight into Sophie's round eyes, and saw them fill and flow with tears. Each crystal (a minute, curved reflection of the room and of Jonny trembling on its surface) was almost immediately lost in the tiny furrows that were part of Sophie's geography. She seemed to radiate a private chill, and Jonny began to shiver, thinking wildly that he had lost his fear of Nev only to become terrified of Sophie. There was nothing comforting he dared to say. She blinked slowly. Then she leaned over and kissed him on the cheek, on the corner of his mouth.

"It breaks my heart," she wept, naked and shivering. "Oh, my darling..."

"Sophie," Jonny said very gently, "don't get cold." The texture of her skin reminded him of the ferny patterns the sea sometimes printed on sand. It could have been beautiful. It was beautiful in its way, that fine print in which no one could read the account of a delicate progress towards an ending. But, as he recorded this possible beauty for later consideration, Jonny shuddered so violently his teeth chattered and his eyes closed with the shock of taking in so many opposites. He dared not move; he dared not breathe.

The unearthly moment passed. He opened his eyes again and stared straight into Sophie's so close to his own.

"Alva," she said, and already there was something doubtful and more commonplace in her voice.

"I'm not him," Jonny said. "I'm just Jonny Dart – you know – the one who looks after you."

"I didn't know you'd changed your name," she said, and Jonny breathed out with relief at hearing a familiar phrase. But suddenly Sophie stood up straight and looked desperately around her.

"Where am I?" she cried loudly. "What is this place?"

"It's home," Jonny said, getting up quickly. "Your home!" he repeated firmly, as she seized his arm, pinching him with passionate alarm. "It's Marribel Road. You know, the house that Errol's father built."

"It's not my home," she said. "I would never live in a place like this."

"Remember Errol?" Jonny cried, as if it were a spell.

"Errol?" she asked in a confused tone, and then said frowning, "Oh, yes. Errol."

"Your husband, Errol West," Jonny said. He remembered teachers at school speaking to him in strong, instructive ways that he was using to Sophie. "Errol West."

"I didn't always like him very much," she remarked devastatingly. "I didn't like his fingernails. But there you are – I wanted to be married. And he turned out to be a dear in a lot of ways." As she talked, she began sounding cosier, more and more like her everyday self. Jonny, tactfully sliding the chair in which he had fallen asleep between them, decided to try shock tactics of his own.

"People say that Errol wasn't very classy," he said. "I mean, he wasn't a professional man, was he?" With great relief he saw her become indignant.

"No, he was not," she cried, "but he was kind and he was honest."

"He never once struck you, did he?" Jonny prompted her.

"He did *not*," Sophie agreed vehemently. "He was one of nature's gentlemen."

"Good old Errol," Jonny said. Sophie nodded slowly, still looking around the room in a measuring way.

"I don't know," she sighed. "You know, everything seemed different a minute ago."

"A minute is all it takes," Jonny said, as Janine fell away from him yet again. It was only now that he noticed Sophie was dragging her nightgown along the floor after her. It looked suspiciously soggy.

"Sophie," he asked her, "have you wet your bed?"

"Someone has," Sophie answered crossly. "I think it's those people next door. They could get a key made, you know, and could just come in here any time they liked."

She looked at him bravely. Her hands and feet looked very large on the end of her thin arms and legs.

"That's all right," Jonny replied in a resigned voice, and indeed he was glad to have the old Sophie back, knowing herself to be old and not fit for romantic dreams. "You sit here by the heater and I'll fix it all up for you."

"I'll make some tea," she offered. "I remember how you like it."

"Don't bother," Jonny said. "I've just had one."

As he searched for sheets that were not too torn to be of any use, Jonny wondered if he had somehow affected Sophie with memories of romance simply by sitting beside her and dreaming of Bonny. When he recalled Sophie's tears, a violent tingle ran between his own eyes and the back of his nose and he nearly wept himself, unable to tell why. It wasn't just out of sympathy for Sophie, though he did feel a confused pity for her. It was more from shock, the shock of coming on an injured animal and thinking you should do something to spare it pain. He thought of the real Alva, whose striped shadow he was, and wondered, as he tried to work out which was the driest side of the mattress, if Alva had loved Sophie enough. Perhaps he had not loved her at all, and perhaps Alva was still alive, sleeping somewhere, old and wrinkled, not even dreaming that his cousin, Sophie, had woken in the night, saying his name and believing herself to be capable of passionate love.

"You're so sentimental!" Janine would have cried scornfully, though she too had dreamed of love, but as something only proper between young people. Could she possibly have been jealous of him, as Bonny had declared?

"You'll never catch me up," she had cried, challenging him, and had vanished before his very eyes.

Jonny helped Sophie into bed, tucked her in firmly, wondering what on earth he could do to save her.

"Goodnight," she murmured. "You're very good to me."

"I'll put the life out," he said, and then stood there, his hand on the switch, chilled at what he had accidentally offered to do. "I mean, the light. It's easier to sleep in the dark." Yet his first offer, though it had been made out of clumsiness, immediately seemed the truer offer of the two. Standing there beside Sophie's bed, he was prepared, for a moment, to believe it was best not to be born than to wind up with broken memories and wet beds. But Sophie smiled the wicked smile she used occasionally, and a distinctly greedy look came into her blue eyes.

"Do you think you could get me some of those sweeties – those whatsitsnames?" she asked him. "I just think I'd like one or two of them."

"Biscuits?" Jonny pulled a stern face. "You want to eat biscuits last thing before going to bed? What about the refined sugar?"

"Just a plain one!" Sophie dropped her voice to a whisper. "Nothing with cream."

Jonny laughed. Sophie's pleasure in the prospect of biscuits set him free, displacing a ferocious moment of truth with a gentle one that was just as true.

"I'll bring the whole packet," he told her. "You can eat them in the dark. Why not, eh?"

She nodded, giving him that look of smiling complicity. But when Jonny came back she was asleep, lying on her back with her mouth open. Her breath was soft and shallow, her teeth were slightly crooked. Another set of teeth lay on the little table beside her bed. Though her eyes were closed, they were not tightly closed. A thin crescent of eye showed between the edges of upper and lower lid. She slept, but not with the sealed sleep of childhood.

Jonny went out into the sitting room, and sat on the settee, his thoughts going to and fro between the old woman in bed and the young one next door. He felt that, in their separate ways, both he and Sophie were in love with ghosts. Bonny had not been the only one to invent the Pythoness. She had sketched an outline which he had filled in with details of his own, and perhaps Sophie, many years earlier, had done the same thing to Alva's striped blazer. Such thoughts flowed through his mind until they were almost indistinguishable from dreams, and it seemed he could feel himself altering under the gentle force of this flow. In the end, tired of trying to work anything out, he went to bed himself, and at last to sleep.

CHAPTER FOURTEEN

The following day Jonny woke to the sound of rain on the roof. The whole city was shrouded in wet mist, so that the one-way street came out of nothing and vanished back into it. From Sophie's balcony window the post office and The Colville pub, their outlines softened by broken films of water, appeared to be melting.

Having seen the rain, Jonny went back to bully Sophie into changing her dress. The one which had mysteriously vanished the day before yesterday had reappeared from somewhere and she had pulled it on over her nightgown. Sophie put up a spirited resistance to changing, but Jonny was firm.

"I'm not going to the shop with someone who's wearing a scruffy nightgown under her dress," he told her.

"I don't tell you what to wear," she replied, but finally gave in and consented to try again. By the time she had taken off the dress, taken off the nightgown, put on a terrible petticoat and pulled the dress on again, she was chattering away quite happily, and offering to make Jonny breakfast.

"Try this first!" Jonny said, peeling her an orange and cutting it into slices.

He thought of Bonny almost experimentally, trying to catch the very first image that came into his mind. There she was – small, freckled, lively, but distant. When he tried to remember the Pythoness he found she no longer existed. All he had was a memory of his own invention and nothing more.

As Sophie ate the orange, Jonny went into the bathroom, bathed and then shaved very carefully. Even a rash would be more respectable than a fine, rough beard that made him look like a reconstruction of prehistoric man. The shirt he had washed yesterday was still damp, though many of its creases had come out over night. Putting it on anyway, he tried to smooth the remaining creases out by hand, reminding himself that most of it would be under the blazer. The face looking back at him out of the mirror was very different from the face that had looked back out of the same mirror only two mornings ago. His swellings and bruises had faded almost entirely, but that was not the only change. Jonny thought he might look older. Wondering what other people might see, he practised smiling, just as he had done when he was small, looked away and then back suddenly, trying to take his face unawares. Frowning, he began to comb his hair, struggling with tangles, flattening its buoyant waves, trying to make himself look rather more subdued and respectable.

It was while he was in the act of trying to flatten it that he succeeded in cornering the new fugitive expression. He could remember it smiling, laughing, looking angry, could remember it furious, or even marked by violent grief, when, alone in his room he had wept for Janine whom he had loved dearly in spite of her small tyrannies. Never before, though, had he seen this calm sadness. It took him by surprise.

"Hey, Sophie," he called. "I look mellow, or something, and I'm only nineteen. How about that?"

"Don't worry! It won't last," Sophie replied comfortably from just behind him, surprising him, for he hadn't expected her to reply. Jonny grinned and blinked. He had left his Walkman upstairs, and it occurred to him that this was the first time in weeks that he had gone into the street without it.

"Sophie, I'm off for a while," he said from the door. She turned slowly towards him.

"You won't be gone long, will you?" she asked him. "It's not much fun being on your own."

"I won't be very long," Jonny reassured her.

"You will come back?" she persisted.

"Don't I always?" Jonny said ruefully. "I'm *programmed* to come back." And he went down the stairs, out on to the street and set off to walk towards the city centre.

The rain was very gentle, sometimes barely a drizzle. The striped blazer kept him warm, and he rather enjoyed walking into such restful greyness and seeing the city change and then change again. Distances were altered. Looking back along Marribel Road and then upwards, he could make out, through the curtains of rain, the rise and fall of the south-east hills beyond the city roofs, the deep clefts curdled with grey-white fog. All around him an eerie bloom appeared on every surface. Not only the post office, but *Cognito Systems* beyond it glowed with a private blush. Jonny wondered what would happen if he went into *Cognito Systems* and tried to order a new memory for Sophie. She would have to be personally fitted, but of course it wouldn't have Errol in it, or Uncle Brian or Jonny's striped blazer. For that matter he might as well put his own name down on the new-memory list himself, for certainly part of his own past had been recorded falsely. Though memories were often regarded as careful files in a catalogue, Jonny now believed they could just as easily be wild stories, always in the process of being revised, updated, or having different endings written on to them. After all, even Sophie's file on Alva was still open, for he, Jonny, was being added to it, even if the entries faded into nothing almost at once.

Jonny wandered on. The Aged Citizen's Council was where Bonny's little map had said it would be. Jonny was almost sorry to arrive. He wanted to go on walking through the restful greyness, enjoying solitude. Now he was at the door he had set out to find, Jonny became irresolute. He walked up and down outside, imagining what *he* might think if he were a social worker and someone like him turned up and told a strange tale of life with Sophie. But he had gone to the trouble of making himself look respectable and it seemed a pity to waste it. Besides, as he hunched his shoulders and stuck his hands into his pockets, he found Sophie's key once more. Taking it out, he held it in his palm and stared at it until it seemed as if key and hand were part of the same thing. With a deep sigh he went up the path and in at a door in the side of the old house.

Beyond the door was an office, and a young woman who smiled at him pleasantly enough.

"I've come to ask about... about a neighbour," Jonny began in a rush. "I live close to her – next to her really – and I think she needs help. She's an old lady – I don't know how old and... someone told me to ask for Mr Dainton, so I..."

But the woman interrupted him.

"I know Mr Dainton's still here, and we might just catch him if we're quick."

"Right," said Jonny, though being cut off in the middle of this first impulsive flow disconcerted him. He followed her down a passage, waiting while she knocked on the door and spoke to someone inside and then, when she stood back and gestured, went into the room.

Jonny thought the man behind the desk looked startled, then resigned, and not altogether pleased to see him.

"I won't keep you long," he began to say, but the man spoke first.

"Well, how are you?" he asked, as if Jonny were an old acquaintance of his. "Feeling better?"

"Better than what?" Jonny replied, taken aback.

"Better than you were the other night," the man said. "You certainly look rather better. I scarcely recognised you for a moment."

"Do we know each other?" Jonny was puzzled. Although willing to believe that he had met this man somewhere previously, he was quite unable to work out when or where.

"I gave you a lift home from Rivendell," the man said. "The last I saw of you you were making quite purposefully for the taxi rank. Right through on-coming traffic, I might add. I saw you get as far as the traffic island, and then I'm afraid I lost my nerve and drove off."

Jonny laughed.

"It seems like another life," he said. "I don't remember anything much about that. I don't even remember you – well, just vaguely now, but not really. Are you Max Dainton?"

"For my sins," the man replied, looking a little more friendly. "If you can't remember who I am or anything about me, what are you doing here? You didn't leave anything in the car, because I checked."

"Nothing to do with all that," Jonny said. "At least it links up, I suppose. I didn't make it to the taxi rank.

Anyhow, I didn't have any money. That was just something I told Bonny's mother. Actually, I flaked out on the traffic island."

Max pulled a face and said he wasn't surprised. Jonny described his meeting with Sophie, and his time in Sophie's house. He did not mention Sophie standing over him weeping for lost love, and he did not mention meeting Bonny, but he did explain his suspicions about Nev. As he talked, Max looked more and more thoughtful. He frowned at Jonny, not in any disapproving way, but as if Jonny were an example of some new species which he had just discovered and was determined to understand.

"Well," he said at last. "That's quite a story."

"Yes, isn't it?" Jonny agreed. "She's a nice old thing. I don't want to walk out on her until I know she'll be OK."

"She's not the only one, you know," Max went on. "There's a lot of them around, out there. And there's nowhere for most of them to go."

"She's got masses of money!" Jonny exclaimed. "She could go into a really nice home and be properly looked after... not that she wants to."

"Money's something," Max said. "A lot of them haven't got any money, although that hoard under the sink you mentioned – that's not uncommon, you know. Still, no matter how much money she's got, there just aren't the places for them. There are three homes in this city that'll take someone like your Sophie and there's a waiting list for all of them. There *is* the psycho-geriatric unit at Sunnyside, of course." (He had named the local hospital for mentally disturbed people. Jonny screwed up his face.) "And there's a waiting list there, too," Max told him, slapping his hand lightly on his desk.

"I can't stay with her for ever," Jonny cried. "She needs to be bathed, and she wets her bed."

"No, of course not!" Max agreed hastily. "If I may say so, you've done very well. A lot of people would have found it much too much to cope with. How have you managed with work?" He broke off. "Oh, you're unemployed, are you?"

"I don't even know what I want to do," Jonny said with a shrug. "I wasn't too hot at school the last couple of years. I'm not qualified for anything."

"Except tap-dancing, apparently," Max said with a grin.

"Oh, yes," Jonny said, grinning back rather sourly. "There's not a big demand. And Chickenbits has been taken over by some Australian gang."

"And you've given up dancing," Max nodded. "I remember you telling Ruth so, very emphatically."

Jonny shook his head. "You remember more than I do."

"They say tap-dancing is making a comeback," Max remarked. "Never mind! I can't come and see Mrs West today, but perhaps tomorrow. Can you stay with her that long?"

"Sure," said Jonny. "I'd better let my mother know where I am, I suppose. I was in a bit of trouble that night I met you, and I've got to appear in court tomorrow. Only the District Court," he added hastily. "My father wasn't too thrilled. He's pretty square."

"I don't think you'd need to be too square to worry about someone in the condition you were in," Max replied. "Have you got a lawyer?"

"They have one there," Jonny said. "It's not as if it's complicated – just breaking the peace and refusing to give my name. I'll turn up and take my chance."

"It's your life," Max said with a sigh.

Jonny felt obliged for some reason to explain something.

"It was five years since my sister died," he said. "She fell over the cliffs at the Seacliff Reserve and, deep down, everyone thought the wrong one had gone over. Dad, too. He couldn't help it."

"You're probably imagining it," Max replied, looking rather harassed.

"*I* thought so anyway," Jonny said. "That was enough, really. But one or two people said so."

He was astonished at himself for telling all this in such an off-hand voice when it had festered in him for five years.

"I'm sure it's not true..." began Max, making the sort of brisk, sensible reply anyone would make. But then he hesitated and looked a little dismayed. Jonny was used to picking up such hesitations.

"Did she say so?" he asked. "Dr Benedicta?"

"She certainly did not," Max replied robustly, but Jonny thought his guess must have come close to the truth.

"Sorry to mention it," he told Max. "I don't let it bother me." Then, anxious to change the subject, he asked, "What's the matter with Sophie, anyway? Is that what being senile is like?"

"She has the classic symptoms of what we now call Alzheimer's disease," replied Max. "Either that, or some associated disorder. It can sometimes attack quite young people, though it mostly affects the elderly. They're doing research on drugs to help it, but they're experimental as yet. There's nothing we can do about it. I'll call and see her in her own home. Is she on the phone?" Jonny shook his head. "Well, if you could stay with her tomorrow I'll try and call sometime during the late morning."

"Don't let her talk you into a cup of tea," Jonny said. "She never puts tea in the pot." Max smiled. They stood up together but, in the hall, Max went one way with a wave of his hand and a cheerful goodbye, and Jonny went the other, past the office and back on to the street again. He had a feeling of anticlimax. Yet he could not have expected that anyone would immediately rush to take over from him at Tap House.

At school he had once been made to read a long poem in which an old sailor (the poem was *The Ancient Mariner)* had shot an albatross and had been punished by having to wear it around his neck. Jonny thought Sophie was rather like an albatross, but with that thought his memory did a surprising thing. It gave him back six complete lines of the poem, lines which had impressed him at the time, but which he hadn't thought about for years.

I saw a something in the sky
No bigger than my fist.
At first it seemed a little shape
And then it seemed a mist.
It mov'd and mov'd and took at last
A certain shape, I wist.

The rain trickled down Jonny's face. He wondered why he had told Max that he should have been the one to go over the cliffs at the Seacliff Reserve. Kept to himself it was a frightening thought, spoken aloud it sounded rather ridiculous and self-pitying. You could begin to make fun of yourself for thinking it. Jonny felt he'd tossed an important part of himself away as if it didn't matter.

Janine had become ash and heat, and heat escaped back into space. Jonny could recall learning that at school. So Janine could never be recaptured. Time being what it was, perhaps alien civilisations in other galaxies were measuring her passing with incredibly sensitive instruments right at this moment. "There goes Janine," they could be crying.

"Still dancing!" All the same it seemed that there was still an empty space in this time and this city into which she would have fitted perfectly, whereas there was no easy space for Jonny, the one who was still alive. He had had to work his way along like a blind man, alternatively guessing and striking out. This was a well-established thought, but now, to his surprise, he detected an odd grating quality in it, as if it had begun to break down.

Jonny had intended to go straight back to Sophie's house, but found he could not bear to do so quite at once. He wandered along the bank of the river, the same one which curved through Colville, watching the surface of the water continually blemished by the fine rain. The air, streaming with the green hair of the willows, looked more fluid than the river. Outside a big hotel, Japanese tourists talked to one another. Jonny smiled doubtfully at them, but they barely saw him. Perhaps they were in a different city from the one he was in. Jonny considered a possible infinity of cities, overlapping, linked only by something like the hotel, or maybe Tap House. For the last three days Jonny had lived in a different city himself. Ordinary things were still ticking over, waiting for him, but Jonny had work to do before he could come back to them.

The rain grew heavier, and the wind began to blow. By the time he got back to Tap House he was chilly, despite the thick blazer. His damp shirt was still drying on him, and his sneakers were soaked. The key was in his hand before he saw that the door was already open a little. Jiggling the key, he stared measuringly at the narrow streak of shadow between the door and its frame. Then he slipped through, stood at the bottom of the stair and listened carefully. Upstairs, Sophie was chattering away busily. There was a sinister absence of cats on the stair. She was not alone. Someone answered her.

Jonny wondered if Max Dainton had somehow found a gap in his schedule and turned up early, but then he heard Sophie saying, "I must have a receipt for this, you know," in a bustling, efficient voice.

"I'll give you a receipt when you give me the money, Mrs West," said a man's voice indistinctly.

All at once, Jonny was filled with a strange and familiar bliss, accompanied by a sense of physical ease. Feeling graceful and filled with power, he moved very softly up the stairs. No matter what changes were taking place in him, no matter what secrets he casually spilled, he believed he was about to lose his temper – and this time for noble reasons. He would give in to the wonderful exhilaration of a good, passionate rage; lose himself in it, and emerge shaken, probably a little damaged, but somehow relieved. Reaching the landing he looked into the sitting room. Sophie's handbag was being violated again, but this time by less sympathetic hands than his.

"That's *my* handbag," Sophie was saying in a spirited tone.

"Is this all you've got?" asked the landlord,

"I never used to pay rent," she complained. "I'm not used to it."

"You'd better pay a bit more next time," he told her. "I own this place now, and if you don't pay rent I'll put you out. I'll have to. It's what Errol would have done. He'd have tossed out anyone who didn't pay the rent. Ask any of the old-timers around here. He was a hard man, Errol West."

"Errol was one of nature's gentlemen," said Sophie. "He would never turn me out of my house."

Jonny was taken aback. He had become increasingly sure that Spike and Nev were the same person, indeed had counted on it. The feeling of fulfilment he had experienced at the bottom of the stairs was partly at the prospect of balancing things with Nev. But Spike turned out to be a weedy stranger, though not quite a stranger. Jonny slowly recognised one of the pair who had watched his encounter with Nev in The Colville pub. He was holding Sophie's bag between his hands as if he were planning to pull it in half. The money she had taken out from the post office the day before lay on the table, while he searched for more. Sophie stood beside him, her right hand making anxious twitching darts at the handle of her bag.

"I want a receipt," she cried in a peevish, parrot-like voice. Spike dropped her bag which fell to the floor – disembowelled and dead – and took a receipt book and a pen from his pocket. At first, neither he nor Sophie noticed

Jonny moving quietly into the room. Then Sophie, turning, saw him, frowned, recognised his blazer and smiled.

"Oh, there you are," she said. "I'm just paying the rent. I won't be a moment." The landlord dropped the pen, spun round, starting when he saw Jonny who was directly behind him, close enough to touch him.

"This is my cousin, Alva Babbitt," Sophie said, introducing him. She used a specially genteel voice for introductions. "This is Mr..." she hesitated, looking at the landlord.

"Lord have mercy, it's good old Spike," Jonny said, smiling and looking happy.

"...Mr Spike," Sophie said. "Sit down, Alva, and I'll make you a cup of tea in just a moment. I remember exactly how you like it."

"Make it now," suggested Jonny. "Maybe Spike'd like one too."

Sophie was rather nonplussed. Clearly the idea of making a cup of tea for a landlord was new to her.

"I must have my receipt," she said at last, and the landlord passed her the familiar pink slip. Jonny noticed with pleasure that his hand was shaking slightly.

"Nice to meet you at last," Jonny said, as Sophie went off into the kitchen. "I've been reading your collected works."

The landlord was not only shorter and thinner than Jonny, he was colder and wetter too, or perhaps he showed it more. His straight, mouse-coloured hair was rather long, and hung in slick streaks around large, pink ears. His eyes were a clear and honest blue. Jonny waited confidently for the warm charge of rage to run through him, but it didn't come. As he waited, the landlord edged around to the other side of the table.

"You're not her cousin," he said accusingly.

"You're not her landlord," Jonny replied. "You've been ripping her off."

"She started it," Spike said quickly.

Jonny had no difficulty believing that.

"You come here every two or three days?" he asked mildly. "That's a bit rough."

Still no rage. He felt indignant and scornful, but nothing more. To his annoyance he even found he was feeling a certain sympathy for Spike. And there was no glory in attacking a false landlord who was smaller than he was.

"She can afford it," Spike replied. "As long as she gets a receipt... she's happy. It was her that *made* me take it in the first place."

"You poor little thing!" Jonny said, playing for time and still hoping for fury. "Made you take it! God, she's a brute, isn't she!"

Spike looked confused. Then he shrugged.

"I used to collect her newspaper money," he said. "It was her idea I was the landlord. I didn't tell her I was."

Jonny saw that collecting paper-money might indeed turn into a habit of collecting rent.

"Did she offer you the radio too?" he asked. "The one you flogged to Nev Fowler?"

"Oh dear, oh dear, oh dear!" said Sophie out in the kitchen.

Spike looked sideways at the money on the table and then back at Jonny.

"Don't even think of it," Jonny told him.

"Who the hell *are* you?" Spike demanded. "You're not her bloody cousin!"

Jonny's rage refused to arrive, but he had felt it often enough to act it out. Taking the edge of the little table he flung it over. The dollar notes fluttered away like paper moths escaping. Spike, suddenly finding nothing between him and Jonny, stepped back in alarm.

"I'm the one that's going to take you apart, that's who I am," Jonny cried, smiling and looking happy. "Get out and don't come back."

Spike hesitated, glancing from side to side. Jonny was between him and the door.

"Get out!" Jonny said again.

Spike dodged left, dodged right. Suddenly he was very frightened of Jonny. Fear made him agile.

"Don't touch me," he shouted desperately. "I've got friends that'll do for you if you touch me."

"If you come here again I'll kill you!" Jonny promised in a savage whisper. He danced on the spot. He made himself look mad. He was strong, but his greatest weapon was his power to be frightening.

Spike darted past him. Jonny heard the rasp of his breath.

"Out!" he yelled after him, rushing on to the landing as the running feet banged frantically on the stairs. But, at the door, Spike turned and shouted back up at him.

"You wait! You just wait."

"I will," Jonny cried down to him. "Any time, mate, any time! You and anyone else." The door slammed.

"You can stop your shouting now," said Sophie cheerfully from behind him. "I've made tea."

Jonny turned, picked the table up again, straightened it, and patted its top. Sophie placed the teapot carefully upon it.

"Oh, there are no cups," she said.

"That's OK," said Jonny. "We'll drink out of our hands." Sophie began to laugh.

"Drink out of our hands," she said. "Oh dear, oh dear! No. I'll get one for you in next to no time."

She went into the kitchen again. Jonny sat at the table and looked around the room. He thought how strange it was that you could learn, from being frightened over and over again yourself, how to be frightening to other people.

"Full moon tonight!" he said, and growled softly. As long as Spike stayed away for a few days there would be time for Max, or for someone like Max, to come and set up some system for protecting Sophie.

"Afternoon tea!" called Sophie triumphantly, though it

really should have been lunchtime. On a large plate she put a cup and an enamel mug. Beside it she placed a small saucer of dried cat food.

"This tea's too weak," she said a moment later, pouring water out of the teapot. Jonny took the enamel mug in a docile fashion. Sophie pushed the cat-food pellets towards him.

"Eat up!" she said in a jolly voice. "Don't worry. Plenty more where they came from."

"Party time for us tonight," Jonny said. "We're having visitors."

"It's a long time to wait until then," Sophie replied, looking at the dried cat food greedily. Before he could stop her she had popped one of the pellets daintily into her mouth.

"Here! Ugh! Stop it!" Jonny exclaimed, disgusted. He seized the dish of cat food and carried it out to the kitchen, but he was smiling as he came back and placed a saucer of biscuits beside her.

"Is it good news?" asked Sophie, smiling wonderingly back at him.

"I've been doing good for others," Jonny told her.

"It's a poor look-out if you can't do something for other people," Sophie agreed warmly. "If you need any help you can call on me. You have to stick together with your own." She took a biscuit with a small sigh of pleasure. "Have one of these," she suggested. "They're very plain. You know, I was reading something the other day – it must have been in the paper – and it said that refined sugar is not good for you." She nodded compellingly at Jonny. "Refined sugar and fried foods."

"It's a dangerous life," Jonny agreed.

"But we must never weaken," Sophie said seriously. "The more the danger, the more the honour. That's what Nana used to say. Do you ever think about the old days?"

"All the time," Jonny sighed. "There's no such thing as the past really. That's what I've worked out. It's always hanging around waiting for its chance to get going again. We've got to fight it, Soph, every step of the way."

CHAPTER FIFTEEN

That particular evening settled down over Marribel Road in clouds of grey rain. The street became a channel down which the autumn southerly roared, driving veils of water before it. The city was stripping itself of its many skins. Soon Jonny, standing on the balcony of Sophie's house, might see its bones showing through. Cars roared steadily by, windscreen-wipers like metronomes, keeping time to the beat of the weather. The storm thumped against Tap House, rattling Errol's sign. Warm and dry inside, flanked by cats, Sophie still shivered, longing to go out to the shops to buy biscuits, but hating the weather. She pattered around the house, searching for a different window, a new one that might open directly into the cloudless blue sky of the cake shop.

"I'll go for you," Jonny offered, but Sophie wanted to go herself. She was addicted to the post office and the magical exchange of a small post-office form for money; she longed for the cornucopia of the biscuit display.

"I have to choose my own," she said.

At last they went together, bowed forward behind Sophie's broken umbrella. Jonny hooked Sophie's arm through his, in case she blew away.

"You are a good guide," she said gratefully, squeezing his arm.

"Train me with kindness and I'll do anything," he told her. "But don't make too much of a pet out of me or I'll chase cats and bite the postman."

"The poor little pussies," said Sophie, indifferent to the sufferings of postmen. "I would never do a thing to hurt those pussies."

Bonny's invitation to dinner, Jonny thought, had been a last-minute kindness as she herded him out of her room of books back towards Sophie's house. His invitation back had been a sort of bravado. However, with chicken pieces, and the right packet of a popular mix for thickening casseroles, he had been known to cook something optimistically called *chicken Provençale*. Fortunately, the package was to be found right next to the packets of instant soup in nearly every grocery shop and supermarket in the world.

Traditional French, tomato-based casserole it boasted about itself in fine print, *flavoured with garlic and delicate herbs. For extra-special occasions, add quarter of a cup of red wine.* Simply reading the description was almost a meal in itself. Once again Jonny ran the gauntlet of The Colville pub (looking right and left for either Nev or Spike as he did so) and bought a bottle of the cheapest red wine available. At other shops, further down the road, he bought potatoes, onions, a green pepper and frozen broccoli, and then sat beside Sophie under the blue sky of the tearoom, patiently watching her eat her cakes. Then they set off home again, worried by the storm which snatched at Jonny's bandit hat and whipped up Sophie's skirts.

"Oh dear, oh dear, oh dear," she cried, torn between laughing and complaining at the rude wind, losing her grip on the umbrella which cartwheeled over and over ahead of them. Cars slowed down and waited tolerantly as Jonny scrambled after it, rescued it and gave it back to her. He found it easier not to try fitting himself underneath it, but every now and then she gave a lunge towards him in a vague effort to hold it over him. He was afraid she might put an eye out.

"I hate the winter," she said, shivering, searching for the key as they stood at her door. "I just dread it."

"Look for the string around your neck," Jonny howled at her over the voice of the wind.

Once inside, Jonny took over the kitchen. He found a casserole dish, chopped the onion and pepper, mixed the contents of the packet with warm water and poured it over the chicken and vegetables. He scrubbed the potatoes. As he did this, Sophie hovered around him, fascinated by his activity, but partly resenting his presence in her kitchen.

She put milk tokens in the teapot and covered them with warm water.

"Is this the right way to do it?" Jonny asked her in a humble voice. Beaming with pleasure at being consulted, she advised him, and Jonny thanked her without following her advice.

"I think it's good for a man to learn how to cook," she observed. "Now, Errol is a very handy man about the place, but he can't cook. And what will happen if he's left on his own? He'll be helpless."

"He'll have to get married again," said Jonny tactlessly. "My dad says a man gives half his food away to get the other half cooked."

Sophie was not very pleased with Mr Dart's robust philosophy. To show her independence she insisted on peeling a potato. Jonny watched her, patronisingly at first, then with increasing admiration. She used a knife, not a potato peeler, but the potato skin came away in a thin unbroken spring, uncoiling from her fingers down towards the counter.

"You're a real craftsman, Sophie," Jonny told her, and she flourished a special knife at him. It had been sharpened so assiduously over so many years it had almost no blade left.

"From the old place," she told him. "It's still good for vegetables. It used to be one of that set of Nana's. We used to have some great old times, didn't we?"

"We'll have another great old time tonight," Jonny told her. "It's nearly party time."

He marched Sophie into her room with the familiarity of an old friend. "Come on – let's get you flossied up. Let's make a dear old lady out of you." Sophie laughed merrily, and helped Jonny sort through her wardrobe. They finally decided on a navy-blue frock hanging among the others in a shroud of plastic. It did not seem to have been worn since she had brought it back from the dry-cleaners, goodness knows how long ago.

"I like navy," Sophie said. "It isn't a colour that goes out of date, and it's – how shall I put it – not too bright. It's always acceptable. If it fits I'll take it."

"I'll leave you to try it on," Jonny said. "I think it will suit you."

He left her, but almost at once she called to him, sounding very distressed. He found her staggering around the room, her arms trapped over her head, twisted in a fine spiral of navy pleats. He had forgotten to unzip the back of the dress for her.

"This material is very nice," she said cheerfully as he untangled her. "It must be easy to wash."

"Yes, but keep it clean," Jonny said. "You've got to do me credit, Sophie."

"It's very good of you to lend it to me, dear," she said enthusiastically. "I will take very good care of it."

"I wouldn't lend it to just anyone, you know," Jonny

pointed out, pulling it straight. She looked a little shrunken in its softly draped top and elegant pleats.

"I think I had a dress like this myself once," she said, smoothing it down. "I think navy's a very acceptable colour, don't you? Not too bright!"

"You need to put on a bit of weight," Jonny said critically. "I'll have to feed you up, Sophie."

"Yes, but there's such a thing as being too fat," Sophie argued. "I was reading the other day that it's not a good thing to carry too much weight."

"I don't think you need to worry, Sophie," Jonny said. "Now, how about shoes? I saw some good ones here the other day." He found a pair of navy shoes wrapped in tissue paper. "There, now! Shoe the horse."

He brushed and combed her hair, parting it in the middle and curling it down around her ears as well as he could. Washed and brushed, free from food stains, she was indeed a dear old lady. Jonny was surprised how being cared for changed her.

"I do look smart," she cried with pleasure, looking at her reflection in the wardrobe mirror.

"Like nature intended," Jonny said, though he knew nature did not really care how Sophie looked. "You look great!" He felt suddenly proud of Sophie, and very fond of her too, but he didn't dare hug her so simply patted her on the shoulder.

"None of that," Sophie said, looking pleased. "Suppose Errol came in unexpectedly."

"If Errol came in unexpectedly I'd be out through that window in a flash – whether it was open or not," Jonny promised her. "Now you come out and watch telly. Don't mess yourself up. Be good."

He hurried into the kitchen to check on the casserole and potatoes. As he did so he thought that, up beyond rolling clouds, the moon would soon be rising and, after calculating carefully, decided it would be a full moon.

"Wolfman's night!" he called to Sophie. "Watch out!"

"That doesn't sound too good, does it?" she answered in a worried voice. "I don't want any wolves getting in here."

"You've got nothing to fear," Jonny assured her. "The wolf's on your side."

He walked back into the sitting room to turn up the sound on the television, and Sophie looked at him with approval.

"I always liked that jacket of yours," she told him. "You've got good taste for a Babbitt. Now, let's call a taxi."

"We're not going out," Jonny explained. "The visitor is coming here."

Sophie immediately panicked.

"I haven't got a thing in the house," she cried, sitting up sharply. "I should have bought some of those nice biscuits."

"We've got enough biscuits to last us seven years," Jonny assured her, walking restlessly into the kitchen then out on the balcony so that he could assess the weather. "Don't you worry about a thing. Even the rain has stopped for a bit."

Though it was wet and cold outside, there was an unexpected gleam of blue in the west between two banks of leaden cloud. It was fresh and clear and cold, with the promise of further rain. As he stood there, looking over the city, he heard a door close somewhere close at hand, turned and saw Bonny on her way to Sophie's house, a large, covered basket over one arm, and a bunch of flowers in her hand. She was wearing – not a jacket or a raincoat – but a wide, green cape which, riding out around her, gave a temporary rippling shape to the wind. Her neck, rising from the collar of the cape, was bare, for she had pinned up her hair quite formally, but the wind snatched strands from under the pins and tangled them around her. Once upon a time, Bonny and Janine used to draw all over the covers of their school exercise-books just such romantic girls, with round breasts and hair like the turbulent manes of wild horses – wild and free on prairies or moors, or on the white beaches of islands in unknown seas... or even, it seemed, in a one-way street.

Jonny ran through the sitting room, down the stairs and opened the door just as she knocked on it.

"Lift up the latch and come in," he said. "Have you brought a basket of goodies for Granny?"

"And for the wolf," she said.

"Full moon tonight," Jonny cried warningly, pointing to the cloudy sky.

"You'll notice I'm not wearing my red hood," Bonny said. "No sense in looking for trouble."

"Good evening," fluted Sophie, looking down from the stairs above them.

"Don't bother to come down, Sophie," called Jonny. "We're coming up. This is Bonny Benedicta. Bonny, this is Sophie West."

"Good evening," said Sophie in a very genteel voice, holding out her hand rather affectedly.

"I'm glad to meet you at last," Bonny said, taking it and shaking it heartily. "We're neighbours. We share the same milkman."

Sophie was delighted.

"I have such trouble with milk," she murmured to Bonny confidentially. "The people next door are always taking it."

"I have the same trouble," Bonny told her. She looked from Sophie to Jonny with an odd expression, inquisitive but doubtful. "What a pretty dress, Mrs West."

Sophie was pleased.

"I always think navy is a very acceptable colour," she said. "It's not – how shall I put it – it's not too bright."

"How about a drink?" asked Jonny, charmed at being host. But Bonny was giving Sophie the flowers, which meant a search for a vase and a fuss about arranging them.

In the basket Bonny had brought two salads and yet another bottle of wine. Jonny was able to find first a corkscrew and then, while Bonny opened the bottle, three ill-matched glasses. Jonny's party was more of a picnic than a party. As he poured the wine, Bonny took off her green cloak and hung it on the end of the curtain rail. It was Jonny's turn to be delighted for, underneath it, she was wearing a silver shirt painted with black moons, and fantastic, baggy trousers in bright stripes of satin. She looked like a cross between Pythoness and clown.

"I really recognise you now," he exclaimed.

"You recognise my clothes," Bonny corrected him. "Not me! On the whole I'm trying to go it alone."

"He seems a nice young fellow," Sophie murmured to Jonny, possibly misled by the trousers.

"Ah, Mrs West, a dipperful of this rare vintage," Jonny suggested, wondering if Bonny were reproving him for more plastic ideas. He offered Sophie a glass of cheap red wine, but not without trepidation. She looked at it dubiously.

"Well, just a drop," she said. "Errol wasn't a drinking man, you know. Just a little at Christmas. He wouldn't take any spirits. Of course, he wasn't Church of England," she ended, as if that explained everything.

"Dinner's nearly ready," said Jonny and sat Sophie down in front of the television, hoping she might be entertained by it and give him a chance to talk to Bonny. However, Bonny began talking before he did.

"I *did* wear these clothes for old-times' sake, because after you'd gone I thought I must have seemed a bit insubstantial. Whereas you..." she broke off. "You know, I only just recognised you."

"I've grown a lot since then," Jonny said.

"I knew you must have grown," Bonny agreed, "but knowing things must have happened doesn't always prepare you for the effect of them. And you looked very..."

"...untidy?" suggested Jonny.

"Disturbing," said Bonny. She thought about it, and then nodded as if she were sure she'd got the right word. "You look like trouble, Jonny."

"Even shaved?" Jonny asked.

"Afraid so," said Bonny. "Have you been taking a course in menace, or what?"

"It would have to be night-classes," Jonny said, intrigued by the possibility. "Actually, I'm much more trouble to myself than I am to anyone else."

Sophie joined in enthusiastically. "He's very kind to me," she said unexpectedly.

"I remember him being kind," Bonny said, gently nodding at Sophie. "Don't look scornful, Jonny! There's not enough kindness going on." But then she held out her arms in a gesture that reminded Jonny of the effigy with which he had danced the evening before. "These are celebration clothes because I've passed in my work, I've met you again, I have a night off, and I've been invited out."

"Terrific," Jonny said, charmed to be, in part, a cause for celebration. "But what about the bloke you were arguing with the other night? Perhaps we should invite him round too?" He did not really want anyone else, but he was curious about the other shadow on the wall.

"Forget him," Bonny answered. "He's out of town."

"Is he married?" Jonny asked suddenly.

Bonny, perched on the end of the settee, looked at him reflectively. "No, he's not. I don't want to talk about him. I've come to talk to *you*." Her voice was decided, but not angry. If anything, she seemed a little flattered at his persistence.

"OK – you suggest something and we'll talk about that," Jonny said, and looked at her expectantly. She did not reply at once, meeting his eyes and smiling as she tried to twist a fallen strand of hair back under one of the pins.

"It ended all too suddenly," she said at last, without explaining what she was talking about, probably knowing she did not need to. "But I should have kept in touch. I meant to."

"Anyhow, your parents were never very keen on bleached hair," Jonny said, surprised to hear how detached he sounded.

"And yours never thought I was quite bleached enough," Bonny replied. Jonny could not deny it. "Oh, well," she said peaceably, "it's hard to get it right, isn't it?" and was distracted by his expression. "Now that's a real tap-dancing smile if ever I saw one. I should think you might graduate top of the menace class."

"Look!" Jonny exclaimed. "If I was being killed, I think I'd hear my mum shouting at me to smile and look happy. I do it out of fear."

"A conditioned reflex," suggested Bonny.

"I will now smile with my conditioned reflex," Jonny agreed. "Actually, it sounds like a camera."

"*My* father enjoyed photography," Sophie said, getting an unexpected grasp of the conversation, "and I used to have a camera. I took some very nice snaps over the years with it. I was good at photography, and I was always good at spelling." Then, with an air of achievement she announced, "Idiosyncrasy!" and looked at them expectantly. Jonny and Bonny waited, nonplussed. Seeing them at a loss she began to spell. "I-d-i-o-s-y-n-c-r-a-s-y!" she spelled triumphantly.

"A big hand for Sophie the wonder-speller," cried Jonny, clapping. Bonny joined in enthusiastically, and Sophie smiled and even bowed graciously, as pleased with applause as any performer.

Jonny had forgotten to warm plates for dinner. He was forced to hold them under the hot tap, one by one, while Bonny dried them for him. It was very companionable standing side by side, rather than face to face. Besides, Bonny had often washed-up in the Dart house. Watching her hands – shy, freckled and wild like thrushes – from the corner of his eye, Jonny wondered if, after dinner, he might persuade her to go to bed with him. Out of this ordinary speculation grew a charmed idea that by making love to Bonny he would get power over her, over the Pythoness and her prophesies, and over the past. He would have it all in a manageable form and it would never get the better of him again.

They set the three warmed plates on the counter to serve dinner. Out in the sitting room Sophie obediently watched the television.

"Oh dear, oh dear, oh dear," they heard her saying. It was hard to tell whether she was complaining or laughing.

"No more bleached hair these days?" Bonny commented. "You've given it up?"

"It was a good instinct back then," he said, dropping hot potatoes on to each plate. "We won the cup. Full marks for striking presentation."

"Very striking, and you were struck for it," Bonny said dryly. "Your mother could have made you match by dyeing Janine's hair your colour. No one would have cared about that."

"Dye Janine?" cried Jonny incredulously. "Dye *Janine?* Are you mad? Dye a natural platinum blonde mouse-brown? Minus ten for style. Don't ring me, Benedicta, I'll ring you."

Bonny laughed, and as they went on talking their voices ran cheerfully together, asking questions, giving answers, sharing old jokes but easily inventing new ones.

They carried their dishes through to the sitting room where Sophie sat, watching an advertisement in which a brand of soap was reminding viewers that it had been proved reliable over many years.

"Remember the good old days?" a woman's voice suggested rather unwisely.

"*I* remember the good old days," Sophie cried eagerly. "I remember the day the bull tried to get into the school playground. We were living in Leeston at the time, and farmers used to drive their stock down the main street. Well, this bull... we were all terrified of bulls..."

Jonny filled his own glass again, topped up Bonny's and added a few drops to Sophie's. Then, thinking of Sophie's navy-blue dress he tucked a tea-towel in at her collar and spread the remains of another across her knees.

"If you drop anything, try to miss the holes," he told her.

"I will," said Sophie earnestly.

Bonny watched him gravely. Jonny was beginning to feel lighthearted, partly because of the wine, but also because he was enjoying himself. He was sure he would not have enjoyed himself if Bonny hadn't been happy too.

"I'm really hungry," she said. "I've been working hard and that means I don't cook. This is a real treat for me."

Sophie leaned towards her.

"Some places you go to," she began, "they aren't – how shall I put it – the quality isn't very *good*. But they go to a lot of trouble here."

"I'll turn the telly off," Jonny said, "and then we can get stuck into an intellectual conversation." As he moved across the room towards the screen an announcer, folded inwards across the eyes by Sophie's set so that he looked highly unreliable, was reading the headlines of the evening news.

"The activist, Hinerangi Hotene and her companion, Boy Reuben, apprehended last evening, have made an initial court appearance in Nelson today," he suddenly announced, just as if he were trying to save himself from being switched off. Jonny paused, his hand extended towards the *off* button, then stepped back again. "There will be more details of these headlines later in the programme," added the announcer smugly. Within the next moment the screen was filled with the large despairing face of a farmer who had slaughtered several sheep in the main street of a provincial town as a protest against current government policy towards farm mortgages. While they stared, he began to weep in front of the cameras.

"Did you know?" Jonny asked.

"I knew she'd been caught," Bonny said. "My mother rang and told me this morning."

"What do *they* think?" Jonny asked again. "My lot would go up the wall."

Bonny carefully cut a potato in half.

"They worry," she said, "but they're on her side. So am I, if you want to know," she added, glancing up at Jonny. "I wish I was more like her."

"Well, go one better," Jonny said. "It's not hard. Throw a cracker at the Prime Minister. Or does that count as me being plastic again?"

"I think plastic is very useful," Sophie said, peering around the table. "Now, I have plastic dishes for cheese and butter, and when they're empty all you have to do is wipe them with a damp cloth and there they are – ready for next time.

"Compared with Samantha I always feel very airy," Bonny said, glancing over at Jonny. "I've always felt colourless. Not outside, of course, but inside – in my head. When we were children I believed Janine's inside colour would rub off on to me and make me vivid, too."

"You've got your own colour," Jonny argued. "It's why I was looking for you."

"Oh, I'm fine as long as I can dress up," Bonny said cheerfully. "I can seem as magical as anyone else. But those black stars and silver moons and things" – she looked down at her painted shirt – "don't sink in under the skin. I want them to go all the way through me."

For some reason, Jonny found this a very sexy thought, but he was distracted by the television suddenly showing a picture of a courthouse and two people being escorted into it. Jonny could not recognise Bonny's sister Samantha in the lean, electric girl who stopped in the door of the courthouse, looked back at the television cameras through her narrow dark-glasses and gave a black-power salute.

Sophie took no interest in the television, simply eating with enormous concentration.

Bonny, now, began to talk – almost dreamily – about her parents who, being idealistic as well as childless, had chosen two daughters whose adoption prospects were not good. "It wouldn't matter now," Bonny said, "because people are waiting anxiously for any baby they can get, but children like me used to have to wait quite a while twenty years ago before being chosen."

"Why?" asked Jonny mystified.

"Well, in my case it was because I'm such a mixture – a mongrel, really," Bonny pointed out. "A little bit of unidentified European, a little bit Maori, some Chinese, a drop or two of Indian, maybe. It's anyone's guess. People are nervous about mixtures. Samantha – Hinerangi, that is – was just a straight Maori-Pakeha cross, but she had a bad harelip though you'd scarcely notice it now." Jonny, thinking back, vaguely remembered an operation and a scar. "We were the next best thing to rejects. But that was the very thing that made us lucky because, as it turned out, that was just what the doctors ordered."

"I'd adopt you," Jonny said. "Wolves do that sometimes. Before I was a Boy Scout I used to be a wolf cub and they used to tell us stories about Mowgli and the wolf pack."

"I don't think wolves should be allowed to adopt babies," Sophie said firmly. "They wouldn't know how to look after them."

"I suppose all parents want their children to match up with their own ideas," Bonny went on meditatively. "I know the doctors really love Samantha and me, but they get a special thrill out of us when we *prove* something – prove that anyone, no matter how hopeless – can be redeemed through love and a good education, I suppose. They want to believe that things can be made better."

"You know, I would never do a thing to hurt those pussies," Sophie said, with the air of someone introducing a startling new topic of conversation. She had finished her dinner and was looking around to see if there was any more.

"Eat up," said Jonny to Bonny. "Mind you, there's no pudding except oranges." As he leaned over and gently wiped gravy from around Sophie's mouth, he was trying once more to recall the Pythoness of his childhood, to imagine her sitting opposite him at this table, authoritative and infallible. But, as Bonny revealed her own uncertainties, the Pythoness became more and more a mere faded puppet with a closed smile, as stiff and clumsy as the effigy he had tried to dance with the night before.

"You see, people think I'm ashamed of being such a mixture," Bonny said, "but I'm not. It's just that I'm not all that *interested* in it. And I know the doctors feel a little bit let down by me, as if I've chosen to live too safely."

"Do they know you walked along under the danger sign too?" Jonny asked. "You could have been the one to fall."

"Even walking under the danger sign I walked very carefully," Bonny replied. "That crack of yours yesterday about having *Winnie-the-Pooh* and then going back to the marae..."

"It wasn't meant to be a crack," Jonny said. "It just occurred to me, and I said it."

"Well, I had *Winnie-the-Pooh* too, you know," Bonny said, "and I seem to be going all the way with Winnie. I've turned out too reliable."

"Your parents don't know how lucky they are," Jonny said. "Mine would love me to be more reliable, but sometimes I reckon I'll go just on – you know – dancing under the danger sign until I fall."

"I think it's important to know when you've had enough," Sophie said, scraping her plate with her fork. "I was reading in the paper somewhere that you shouldn't eat too many fats or refined sugars. They're not good for you."

"Of course, it's sort of fascinating there," Jonny added, still thinking of the danger sign. "That's why it's hard to move on." Distracted by Sophie, he missed the thoughtful look Bonny gave him.

"Coffee," he said, "or tea?"

"We'll do the dishes first," Bonny suggested. Sophie leaped to her feet.

"It's much easier in the morning if you tidy up the night before," she said confidently.

"You sit down, Soph!" Jonny told her. "There aren't

many dishes. That's one thing. And I don't think there are any tea-towels. That one we used earlier is wet, and the ones you're wearing are full of holes."

"That's funny." Sophie frowned in a puzzled fashion as she sat down. "I've got plenty of tea-towels. There are the ones Mavis gave me when we got married, and I bought some at the kitchen sale in town." She swivelled around to stare at him sharply. "Do you think those people next door have got my key?" she asked. "They could have a copy made and just come in here and take anything they liked. Where's my handbag?" Jonny sat it on her knee, and she began to sort through it anxiously.

"You think you've got problems with your neighbours," he said to Bonny. "You should hear what we have to put up with."

As he washed the dishes, and Bonny did the best she could with the tattered tea-towel, he told her about his visit to Max Dainton. Through the kitchen door he could see Sophie falling asleep, gradually slumping forward over her handbag, one arm dangling limply towards the ground. While he heated water for the coffee, they drank the last of the wine and Jonny described his altercation with Spike.

"There's another example," said Bonny. "You've only been here a few days and there you are rescuing elderly gentlewomen and fighting off villains. I've been here a year and all I've done is to write about two-thousand essays."

"You wouldn't really like to be me, though," Jonny replied. "I've thought about it a lot, on and off. I mean, I've kept on going. I've finished school – not that I did very well – and I've made some friends. I play with a band when the drummer can't make it, but really I just drift around and it's like I said a minute ago. I'm stuck back there. Janine fell and you hugged me and nothing's happened since. Not until now."

"What's happened now?" Bonny asked. Yesterday's amused look had gone. She was interested, perhaps a little disturbed by what he was telling her and, though she was holding a plate, she had stopped drying, waiting for his answer.

"I'll show you a trick," he said, casually taking plate and tea-towel from her. Then he put his arms around her and kissed her. Bonny looked at him disbelievingly. He had the feeling that she might be about to laugh at him. He kissed her again and this time felt that she was on the point of kissing him back. However, she did not quite do this.

"Come on! Be unreliable," Jonny whispered. "I'll help you. I'm in practice." But, without actually struggling, Bonny somehow managed to grow angular and defensive in his embrace.

"It's not a good idea," she said rather breathlessly. "It gets too complicated."

"Wrong!" Jonny declared. "It gets simple."

"No," she said.

"Why not?" Jonny asked. "I'm colourful. My colour might rub off on you. It might go all the way through."

"It's a threatening colour," she said, smiling but shaking her head. "It doesn't suit me."

"Purple?" Jonny said, thinking of his bruised eye. "It's the colour of kings. It makes us royal."

"No," she said, and tried to move away from him. But Jonny, remembering her first hesitation, believed that if only he held her, though she might go through the forms of anger and struggle and beat against him, in the end, when he touched her, she would give in. So they fought in Sophie's kitchen. Jonny, with his right hand on her breast, pressed himself against her rather as Nev had once pressed against him, and suddenly her silver blouse with the black moons on it tore harshly. The sound of the tear did what her words and her struggling could not do – filled him with dismay, and made him let her go.

"Damn!" said Bonny, looking down at the tear, but making no attempt to pull it together again. She did not try to cover herself, but she did not look at all provocative. It was as if he had suddenly become so insignificant she did not need to hide herself from him. "Why did you have to do that?" she cried scornfully. "I was enjoying being with you, and now it's all spoiled."

"I've followed you," Jonny cried. "I thought – I don't know what I thought. I thought you'd tell me something true." As he said this he knew it sounded ridiculous. He could not explain, even to himself, how wanting to go to bed with Bonny Benedicta could possibly have anything to do with being told something true. But the unexpected word "true" caught Bonny's attention and she suddenly crossed her arms over her breasts, staring at him incredulously.

"True?" she cried, catching her breath, and then smiling as inscrutably as any Pythoness. "Well, you'll never know now, will you?"

Sophie stirred and jerked upright in her chair, twitching like a dreaming dog.

"I'll make one in just a moment," she murmured.

Bonny tried to put her cloak over her shoulders without letting her torn blouse fall open. Jonny watched her. He thought he should apologise, but all words seemed inadequate. Besides, both he and Bonny knew he was not sorry in the way he should have been.

"Shall I help you?" he asked.

"Don't come near me," she cried, and flinging the cloak over one shoulder ran down the stairs, just as Spike had done earlier in the day. Jonny did not try to follow her. He stood transfixed, listening to her rapid, retreating steps and the door slamming.

"Where have you been? " asked Sophie sleepily.

"Nowhere," he replied slowly. "And I'm not going anywhere."

In his thoughts, he embraced Bonny again, and lived once more the first half-second when it had seemed she would give in, imagined her growing soft, putting her arms around him, agreeing to climb the stairs with him.

"I'm going to bed," Sophie announced.

"Remember Uncle Brian!" Jonny said. "I'm not safe company."

"I shall barricade my door," she cried quickly.

"A good idea," said Jonny warmly, and growled softly. Sophie looked alarmed.

"None of that!" she said with great displeasure. "I don't know what your mother would say."

"I do! She'd say 'Smile!'" said Jonny, and smiled.

"You come from an unreliable side of the family," Sophie declared from her bedroom door, and Jonny agreed.

"I'm not too bright, but I'm not even acceptable," he remarked. "I'm not even navy-blue."

"You always meant well," Sophie assured him through the crack in her closing door. Then she pulled the door closed, leaving Jonny wondering for the first time if this was indeed true.

CHAPTER SIXTEEN

With no company except himself Jonny walked up and down and around the room, moving from the door to the landing, between the television set and the desk, to the door of Sophie's room and back again. The cats, crouched in their corners, watched him from slitted eyes. Although it was only about ten o'clock it felt like midnight, or even later. It felt as it had felt the night he came to Sophie's house, like a time outside ordinary time. This particular *now* would never record itself on any clock. Jonny had an intimation that his time here was over. He had started out with timelessness, and had come back to it. The circle was closing up.

In the corners of the ceiling spiders checked the frail grey braces they had built between ceiling and wall. Jonny had pursued the Pythoness to her cave, but he could not possess her or the power she stood for.

Tearing her moon-blouse did not subdue him. On the contrary he felt charged with wildness, partly because he had not been forgiven. Pacing the room, like a wolf pacing a cage, he turned his face to the ceiling and howled silently at the moon riding somewhere high above the clouds. He did not want to struggle with his own overcharged thoughts any more and tried to drive them out of his mind by filling the spaces they might try to occupy with the music of the band.

"RIDING THE NOWHERE ROAD," they sang, right as usual. Jonny walked through the kitchen and out on to the balcony to stand in the cloudy river of wind streaming towards him down Marribel Road. Next door, Bonny's light picked out the line of her balcony rail. "RIDING THE NOWHERE ROAD," the band repeated, and gave out a series of animal cries, yelps and barks.

"Ruff!" agreed Jonny, barking quietly. Down the road The Colville was sending its last patrons out into the rain. He could see the pale yellow stain of light spreading across the pavement and losing itself as it came into the dominion of the street lights. He could hear distant, cheerful voices. A single constant stream of water fell on the middle of the balcony. Jonny worked out that, due to some fault in the old spouting, water was discharging along the tap. It flowed as if it were connected to an infinite system.

"Tap-dancing," Jonny said, and laughed aloud. He did a step or two which carried him through the stream of water to the very front of the balcony, then back under it to the doorway again.

"MAN OF THE HAPPINESS SCREEN," sang the band in sinister voices.

"Actually, it wasn't too bad," he told them, as they sang on. "I'd do it again but I've lost the trick." How could you find your way back to the rhythm in the heart of things? You could knock patiently at the door of that heart, shout jokes through the keyhole or beat on it in rage and try to force it open, and it would still shut you out.

"OK – come on!" he said to the tap. "Baptise me while you have the chance. Make me all new... I dare you."

As he danced under the stream of water he looked up Marribel Road and saw the white van turning round the corner by The Colville pub. Glancing in this direction at that moment was quite accidental, but this accident gave him the chance to step back into the doorway before either the headlights or the ambient light of the city betrayed him. He pushed the headphones back away from his ears as he dropped to his knees, and, though he could not see the van any more, the roar of its damaged exhaust enabled him to track its progress. He was not surprised – was almost gratified – to hear doors open and close and to know that Nev was looking for him.

"The light's on!" said a low voice.

"Get out of the rain," said another, not bothering about who might hear. That was Nev speaking, quite confident in Colville, his home ground. There were three visitors on the pavement in front of Tap House. Feet shuffled as they moved in quickly under the protection of the balcony.

"Let's forget it!" the first voice said. "Face it, Nev – if there's any trouble, Don's in the wrong."

"There won't *be* any trouble," said Nev. "Take my word for it. Once this guy knows I'm on to him, he won't be able to get out of here quickly enough." His voice was monotonous – droning and sinister, just as Jonny remembered it. Partly by listening, partly by guessing, partly because he had tuned himself into Nev's way of thinking and speaking, Jonny understood every word. "He isn't any relation of old lady West... His lot lived here for a while, years ago. I'd know if he was anything to do with the Wests."

"He's just as bad as me," said a third voice Jonny recognised as Spike's, whose real name must be Don. "Hey, Nev – let it ride! I don't want no trouble. I don't care."

"*You* don't care," Nev said contemptuously. "Well, I bloody *do* care. You don't know that sort like I do. I remember when he came here before, him and his sister, stuck-up bitch, walking around Colville like Lady Muck. She just thought she was too bloody good for the rest of us, the great television star, and only on bloody ads, too. I'd have too much pride to advertise pieces of chicken. As for him in there, he used to be so scared of me he'd wet himself if he saw me coming. Knock on the door, Don. If he comes, just leave it to me. I know just how far I can go."

Jonny, impressed with the hissing intensity of Nev's voice, understood that like anyone else Nev was touched by memory... the memory of Janine who had exercised power over him simply by ignoring him. Somewhere from a long way up Marribel Road a car came roaring towards them, travelling much too fast as it braked at the traffic lights.

"Yeah... well, suppose the old lady answers the door," said the first voice.

"She doesn't know if it's day or night, eh?" Nev pointed out. "Say we've come to read the meter, and go past her. You could do anything to her and she'd have forgotten it by morning."

"Well, suppose he goes to the cops?" asked the first voice.

"I reckon he's a bit dicey himself," Nev replied. "He looks spaced-out."

Jonny stood up very carefully, waiting for the noisy car to roar off again. He could hear it grumbling down the road. Then the lights changed and several cars moved, one of them accelerating alarmingly, swinging out into the next lane to pass the truck ahead of it. His movement masked by the sudden action, Jonny swung himself softly and nimbly up on to the flat rail that ran around the balcony and, looking down, saw the three men clustered around Sophie's door almost directly below him. Don knocked nervously. Nev told him not to be feeble and himself banged more commandingly. There was an intensification of the light from Bonny's kitchen window, but Jonny barely noticed it. He was concentrating on the enemies below and on his precarious balance. They banged on the door again.

Jonny cleared his throat.

"Hey, Nev! Up here," Jonny called. The tight cluster below him broke apart convulsively. They turned their faces up to him.

"Chickie?" Nev exclaimed. "Is that you, Chickie?"

Jonny took a breath.

"Chick-chick-chick-chicken!" he cried, balancing – even dancing – on the flat rail.

"Come on down!" Nev urged him. "We just want to have a word with you." But he was nonplussed by Jonny's materialisation there above him.

"I'd be mad to come down, wouldn't I?" Jonny cried. "Three of you. One of me!"

Nev was silent, wiping the rain from his eyes.

"You'll come down if you're really that worried about old Mrs West," he said at last, speaking once more in his flat, monotonous voice. "She's got a hell of a lot more to lose than a few dollars a week. You can just walk out, but she's stuck here, isn't she?"

"Hey, Nev," said the unknown man uneasily. From up above, Jonny could barely tell one face from the other.

"You threatening her?" Jonny asked.

"Just read the papers," Nev said. "See what happens to a few other old people. They have all sorts of accidents."

"Oh, gee, Nev! You're so ruthless," Jonny said mockingly, gathering his forces.

"Come down and have a word about it," Nev said. He waited. "Come on, Chickie," he persisted. "Remember, your family doesn't have a good head for heights."

Jonny flung his arms wide and cried out in the very echo of Janine's single cry. The saved energy of the leap he had not taken five years earlier filled him, and he leaped now as if he might fly. Wet, gleaming surfaces, moving lights, the three up-turned faces all rushed towards him, while he saw, not through these things or beyond them, but indivisibly built into the same space, the sea, the rocks, the red dress wound across by disintegrating snakes of foam. "Smile!" his mother reminded him, as he fell towards the city, and he did smile, for falling towards the city he fell into the sea.

I'm going to be killed, he thought as he fell. It's about time.

Jonny came down among the three men with alarming force, cracking Nev in the face with his foot, more by accident than good management, glancing against one of the other two – he was not quite sure which one – and finally slamming against the wall beside the door so violently that he rang with the impact and was momentarily stunned and blinded by it. He was quite helpless for a second, but it did not matter. So was everyone else. Two of his enemies were rolling on the ground, and the third, Don, the landlord, stood staring and gaping. Nev, tough as ever, scrambled to his feet, cradling his face in both hands, while the other man dragged himself on to all fours, then to his feet. Jonny took a breath, and since it was a public performance, looked happy.

"Jeez! He's mad!" cried Don. He sounded terrified, but if so, terror made him come at Jonny swinging, striking him on the side of the face. Jonny felt the blow, but only as if it fell on someone else. He leaned back against the sturdy wall of Sophie's house, swung his foot between Don's stomach and his chest, and thrust him back across the pavement and out into the road. There was a tooting of horns and the sound of quick braking.

Nev was coming towards Jonny, not fast, but very deliberately indeed. He was still holding his face with his left hand. Jonny imagined the shadowed eyes looking out over that hand would be murderous. And now he made an alarming discovery. One of his arms, the one which had taken the force of the impact, would not work properly. He could lift it a little but certainly no higher than his shoulder, and Nev was on him. Yet, in the very moment when he might have destroyed Jonny, Nev stepped back, dropped his left hand and revealed a face twisted not only by pain, but by such horror, that Jonny turned involuntarily to see what had horrified him.

The green door was open and coming out of her box of darkness was Sophie, armed with the hearth brush, and resplendent in her petticoat, suspender belt, crimson hat and one shoe. Over one arm she carried her handbag. She looked like an old, old spirit, her thin silver hair turned into a phosphorescent nest by the street light, her eyes nothing but two black holes under her high forehead, her mouth bursting with more teeth than any natural mouth could hold. Her lips were stretched thin trying to accommodate the impossible number of teeth, teeth which extruded over her lower lip, making it seem as if she were beginning to devour herself.

Involuntarily, Jonny flung up his own good arm as if to defend himself. Before he could remind himself that it was only Sophie, every nerve in his body told him to put himself out of mortal danger. He took a step forward and, since he could not strike Nev, embraced him furiously with his good arm. Recovering, Nev thumped at his back, trying to tear free. They wrestled and beat each other to the pavement where they rolled over and over like two of Sophie's cats, inextricably locked together, first Nev, then Jonny, on top. Every jolt to his shoulder filled Jonny with such pain he almost fainted, but he still seemed to be bearing it for someone else. At one moment he vaguely saw Sophie bent over them like a fury, beating Nev with her hearth brush. Then it was Jonny's turn to be on top. Getting some purchase with his knees, tangling the fingers of his right hand in the crown of Nev's hair, he banged Nev's head on the pavement.

"Don't you touch me again," he shouted. "Don't you ever touch me again."

"He's mad! He's mad!" someone was shouting. Nev's body arched desperately under his. Jonny was dislodged and rolled over once more. Nev kneeled over him, still trying to hold his own face with one hand as if he thought it might fall apart. He struck at Jonny, but there was no more power in his blow than there had been in Jonny's and he did not try to repeat it. He just glanced up, and then remained kneeling, staring, bathed in an eerie, flashing blue light. Jonny suddenly flung his arms wide, gasping at the charge of pain on the left.

"Nev," he croaked. "This is so sudden. I didn't know you cared."

Then he began to laugh. He laughed and was still laughing when someone laid hands on Nev and pulled them apart. It was a police officer. A second one bent over Jonny, who kept on laughing. He laughed as he stood up and stared around him at a whole audience. Cars had stopped; interested strangers had materialised. Bonny was standing there with her arm over Sophie's shoulders. Sophie still looked horrific, but Jonny understood by now that she had simply jammed an extra top set of teeth over the ones she normally wore. Don and the unknown third man were both talking wildly to the officer holding Nev.

"Just take it easy for a bit," said Jonny's guardian, but he was looking at Sophie not Jonny. Almost everyone was. Bonny spoke to her and turned her very gently towards her doorway. Sophie nodded, putting both her hands in Bonny's, and they vanished into her dark box. A moment later, Bonny reappeared alone and looked towards him.

"I'd say you just might have a broken jaw," Nev's policeman was saying to him. "I think we'd better run you along to the casualty department."

"Hey, Bonny," Jonny called, and she came over to him.

"You see..." he began haltingly, "sometimes I think I pushed her, I sort of remember doing it."

She came a step or two towards him.

"Pushed who?" asked the officer alertly, looking up at the balcony. "Not the senior citizen!"

"You know you didn't," Bonny said in a very matter-of-fact voice. "Really, you must know you didn't."

There was a lot of talking going on, Don and his companion both interrupting one another, pointing at Jonny and Nev, the other casual audience talking among themselves, probably hoping for more drama. Words had passed between Bonny and Jonny almost privately. And now Jonny, having felt nothing, felt everything... the rain that trickled down his face and neck, the hand on his arm and the pain in his shoulder – a pain that was suddenly so much his own that he winced and cried out with it as if it had only just been inflicted. He did not see how he could ever have held it at a distance.

"It just seemed I must have pushed her," he said, "because you said I should say I was with you." Then he began to talk very quickly while it was all clear in his mind, everything running together and pouring out, there under the balcony of Sophie's house. "I *thought* of it. I was actually thinking of grabbing her when she said that about me never catching her up. It didn't mean much, it didn't mean anything, but then she just... she just vanished. I knew I must have done something to make it happen... well, not *knew*, I just *believed* I had. I could remember not doing it, but I could remember doing it, too."

"I thought it was going to be terrible for you," Bonny cried softly. She looked haunted. "I thought you had enough to cope with. I wanted to protect you, that's all. But she tripped. She tripped and fell."

They stared at each other.

"Once you start thinking something like that," Jonny stammered, "how do you stop? It makes itself real." And then quite naturally he went from laughing to weeping, falling on to his knees, weeping still, as the substance of whatever had been holding him together dissolved away.

"We'd better get this bloke to the doctor," the officer was saying to Bonny. "He's done himself some damage. You did the right thing to ring us, but God, who'd be a cop!" They were putting Nev into the first car; someone was opening the door of the second car and looking at Jonny. "Come on, mate. We haven't got all night."

"OK folks, the show's over," one of the policemen was saying.

"I'll be all right in a minute," Jonny said, thinking he would be, but he wept on. The sea he had carried inside him for so long tried to make itself one with the outside sea, the same one that boomed on the rocks at Seacliff and roared invisibly at the foot of Sophie's house. "Give me a moment," Jonny said, lying face down on the pavement so that all shameful tears would be hidden. But, hot as tea, they kept on flowing, dropping on to the pavement outside Sophie's house and becoming an indistinguishable part of the wet film that covered the pavement at Sophie's door.

CHAPTER SEVENTEEN

One Friday evening, six weeks later, Jonny sat among the bushes on the traffic island once again, watching the constant streams of cars sweeping over the motorway and peeling off, left and right, into the city. He was wearing his striped blazer, bandit hat and Walkman, but the battered creature who had once woken up there in the small hours of the morning had become yet another ghost, haunting memory. A different Jonny was on his way back to Sophie's house. By beginning here he was making his mysterious adventure hold its tail in its own mouth, like the serpent on Bonny's ring.

He stared at the city for about ten minutes, the top of his head barely showing above the leafy tops of the bushes.

"TURNING ON THE WHEEL – TURNING ON THE WHEEL IN THE AIR," sang the band, and Jonny, who had been waiting for their instructions, got up, picked up the bag at his feet, and crossed over to the corner where three streets came together, choosing the street which began with well-kept shops but decayed into a series of smaller, meaner establishments. From here he moved between loading bays and fences of steel pipe (THIS PROPERTY IS PROTECTED BY CITYGUARD SERVICES, said a notice), and then through the supermarket car park past people pushing great trolley loads of provisions to their cars. Everyone appeared to be preparing for a siege.

Jonny went into the supermarket, bought a packet of biscuits, another of dried cat food, some flowery wrapping-paper and Sellotape. A little later he sat down on the edge of the Marribel Road footpath, ignoring the wheels and the busy feet turning and tapping before and behind him, and carefully wrapped both the biscuits and the cat food so that they looked like presents.

As he did this, the fierce insect-voice of a fire engine began to wail, coming closer and closer all the time. Recently the sound of fire sirens had made him imagine Sophie's ironing board, burning and twitching in the flames. But this evening he knew she was not alone and, though he automatically looked up, trying to find just where the sound was coming from and where it was going, it was just another one of the many things happening around him.

As he walked down Marribel Road, three fire engines rushed by him, flashing and screaming. Jonny obeyed the traffic signals meticulously. Passing the old Colville post office, he stopped to read a notice on its door, explaining that tenders were being called for the building of a new modern post office close to the supermarket. On the wall beside it was another notice, urging people to protect the heritage of the city and to protest against the demolition of buildings such as this one. There was a printed signature: Harold Fowler (Councillor).

The pub on the opposite corner was as busy as ever.

Only last week Jonny had come face to face with Nev in the city square. Jonny's father believed, or said he believed, that a good fight cleared the air, and he had folktales of his own youth in which he had fought (and beaten) some enemy who had turned out to be "a heck of a good joker" and, subsequently, a life-long friend. Jonny knew that he and Nev would never have such feelings about one another. All the same, when he remembered trying to win Bonny by force, or coveting the money he had found under Sophie's kitchen sink, and when he imagined living in Colville, and finding one's empire slipping, day by day, into a new and largely inaccessible form, he understood something about Nev that took the edge off savage memories. Neither of them had won in their recent fight, but at least he had shown that he had got beyond fear, to become fearsome.

"Hi, Chickie," Nev had said.

"Jonathan, to you," Jonny corrected him. Nev looked as if he might add something, but then he shrugged, smiling faintly and turned away with an odd wave of his hand, saying goodbye to some dream of which Jonny was only part, a dream of something that had never been his. Jonny felt they would meet again from time to time but without the will or interest or energy to fall on one another again. There was no sign of Nev or his van around The Colville pub tonight.

Tap House was in front of him, its tap dry, the windows over its balcony lit. When he reached it he did not knock on the door at once but sat down on the edge of the footpath, reached into his bag and began to change his shoes. Jonny's hair tossed in the wind as he took a small tape-recorder from his bag. Putting both bag and tape-recorder in the angle between the pavement and the wall of Tap House, he stood under the balcony and yelled.

"Sophie! Hey, Sophie!"

There was no response. He yelled again.

"Sophie!"

This time, there was an alteration in the light. Shadows moved up beyond the window, then the balcony door opened, and Bonny led Sophie out on to the balcony.

"Bring out that angel of wisdom!" he shouted.

"Who is it?" he heard Sophie asking.

"You've got an admirer," Bonny replied.

"Oh dear, oh dear, oh dear!" cried Sophie, chuckling and a little agitated. He could see she was wearing the tea-cosy on her head.

"Hey, Sophie!" he cried. "Look at me!" Darting in under the balcony he switched on the tape, and the music of his little sisters' competition piece came thinly out into the darkness of Marribel Road.

"When the red, red robin
Comes bob, bob, bobbing along…"

sang a light, male voice against a background of passing cars. Jonny, singing along with it, began to dance. Bonny and Sophie, staring down over the balcony rail, watched him change into a surreal man whose feet stuttered like typewriters, though the story they wrote down vanished as soon as it was told. It was too shy a story – too full of contradictions which cancelled each other out – to stand being put into words. In the very moment of being communicated, Jonny's story disappeared.

"Wake up, wake up you sleepyhead,
Get up, get up, get out of bed,
Cheer up, cheer up, the sun is red,
Live, love, laugh and be happy…"

sang the singer, sang Jonny.

"I love this good old song," Sophie remarked somewhere above him. And the sky really was red, but not with the sun. Just as if the city were mocking the song, the sky behind Jonny blushed with the dull, angry glow of a big fire which, shining on the clouds of its own smoke, gave a ruddy, curdled appearance to the air behind *Industrial Gloves*.

> *"I'm just a kid again,*
> *Doing what I did again,*
> *Singing a song.*
> *When the red, red robin comes bob, bob, bobbing along,"*

Jonny sang, grinning derisively to himself, dancing something opposite to the bright, optimistic words, flinging his arms wide, leaning sideways into the air. The song stopped. Jonny and the music stopped together.

Up on the balcony Sophie and Bonny cheered and clapped. On the other side of the road, quite unexpectedly, there was more clapping. Jonny turned and saw a woman and two children staring at him and applauding. He waved to them and they waved back. Bonny left the balcony.

"Is that you, Alva?" Sophie called down to him.

"It's Jonny Dart," he shouted back. "You won't know who I am." The green door opened and Bonny beckoned him in. She had been expecting him, because he had rung her earlier.

"Hello," Bonny said. "How are things, Jonny Dart?"

"Things are fine," said Jonny, looking around. The

supermarket trolley was gone. Someone had vacuumed the foot of the stair, had polished the hand rail. There was an unexpected brightness about everything.

"Higher power," Jonny said, not talking about any spiritual effect but about the light bulb in the landing light. "I could have done that."

"You can't think of everything," Bonny said. She was wearing black corduroy trousers and a blue jersey. Her hair was tied back from her face with a narrow, black ribbon.

He followed her up the stairs and into the sitting room, where Sophie came to meet him.

"How did you get in?" she asked him.

"You gave me the key," Jonny said. It was true. He still had the key to Sophie's house in his pocket.

"You've come just in time," she said, beaming at his striped blazer. "I was just going to make a pot of tea and have some of those cakes."

"Great! I'd love one," said Jonny, looking around the room and then back at the tea-cosy she was wearing. She needed a spout coming out of her forehead to set it off properly. "Terrific hat, Sophie. Take it off and let me have a good look at you."

Sophie removed the tea-cosy. Her hair looked quite different, for it had been washed and was white, shining and fluffy – except where the tea-cosy had flattened it. She was wearing a clean, checked skirt and the blouse with the paisley pattern that he himself had once selected for her.

The cobwebs were swept away; the cat hair that had matted the cushions was gone. All the wooden surfaces were dusted and polished. Jonny knew, because he had kept in touch with Bonny by phone over the past six weeks, that Max Dainton had called and talked to Sophie. He had arranged for a district nurse to call in once a week to bath Sophie, and for another woman to come and tidy the house. But he had not imagined how different it would look.

There were several cats in the room, cats that he recognised from last time, but even they had become cosier, more respectable. They were curled up compactly, watching everything as smugly as if they had brought about all changes for the better themselves. With relieved nostalgia Jonny saw a cake of soap in one pigeon-hole of the desk, orange peel in another, and half a pair of false teeth in the third. He felt reassured by this, for the old disorder had become filled with a sort of romance. Though he did not really regret its passing, he remembered the first night in this house when it had seemed he had cut through the defences people put up against natural anarchy to the true disintegrating centre of things. Of course, one didn't have to submit to that kind of disintegration, but it did no harm to be reminded it was always going on. He put his arms around Sophie and hugged her, looking at Bonny over her shoulder.

"How are you getting on, Soph?" he asked her.

"Not too badly," she told him. "The young fellow there

looked in. I've been giving him a hand. I think it's a poor thing if we can't help out, don't you?"

"What about me?" Bonny said. "Don't I get a hug?"

It was not only a way of telling him he was forgiven, but a way of pointing out she was not afraid of him.

"Sophie says you never know what that sort of thing will lead to," Jonny said, as he kissed her cheek.

"It doesn't have to lead anywhere," Bonny said. "It can be the place you arrive at. And tea is almost made."

Jonny knew that Bonny had taken to calling in on Sophie, either to share her dinner, or, if that was too inconvenient, to make a proper cup of tea for her afterwards.

"You sit down," Sophie said. "I'll bring it in for you in just a brace of shakes." She went out, followed by Bonny. Jonny, feeling like a visitor, sat down, turning the tea-cosy over and over. The doll with the broken face smiled half a smile at him.

The television had been adjusted. The horizon no longer devoured its own black-and-white ghosts. Flat and relatively undistorted, they moved busily backwards and forwards telling a story of humorous misunderstandings.

Bonny came back into the room carrying a tray with tea and biscuits.

"I've brought presents," Jonny said, and gave Sophie two parcels to open.

"Is it my birthday?" she asked.

"Near enough," Jonny said. He looked over at Bonny. "I'm sorry about tearing that shirt," he said. "I mean, I really am, I didn't say so at the time."

"I probably wouldn't have worn it again, anyway," Bonny said. "How's your shoulder?"

"As good as new," Jonny said. "It was only dislocated. I came a hell of a crack against the wall. It's just as well Errol's father used the best wood and the best nails."

"And what about everything else?" Bonny asked. "Is everything else mended?"

Jonny knew she must be talking about the strange, wrong conviction that had grown on him slowly – a parasitic dream feeding on other guilty dreams that he had pushed his sister from the ridge below the danger sign to clear the way ahead for himself.

"It's funny," he told her, "it seemed truer than a lot of other things that really were true. It was like, you know – sometimes you *know* you've switched the heater off, and yet you've still got to go back and check. You go back into the house thinking what a fool you are, but you still have to go back." He waited for Bonny to say something, but she only sighed, smiled and shook her head. "Maybe there's another life going on at the same time as this one," Jonny said speculatively. "Another life, almost the same, but not quite, and everyone does things a bit differently in each one, but only knows about them one at a time. Maybe I *did* push Janine in some other life, and somehow it all leaked over into *this* one."

Bonny listened, and Jonny was pleased by that single stare, and pleased with his own words. He had thought of them often enough over the last fortnight as he pushed wheelbarrows full of clay, but he had never spoken them aloud until now. "I read that idea in a science-fiction comic," he concluded.

"I think reading is a very nice hobby," Sophie said with the air of someone putting forward a revolutionary idea. She was still trying to unwrap her parcel. "You can learn a lot from reading. My father did a lot of reading, and not just light stuff. He used to read very hard books."

"Yeah, well, he was an MA, wasn't he?" Jonny said. "He would go for something from the top shelf. Just tear that paper off, Soph, or you'll never get it open."

"Oh, I always save the paper," Sophie said.

Bonny still said nothing.

"It used to get at me last thing at night," Jonny explained, "or if I was very happy about something, or if I'd been drinking. You see – Janine always seemed more *alive* than I did, didn't she? You said she was 'vivid'. And then – you and me – we did tell that lie. I was really grateful at the time, but after a while I began to think there must have been some special reason." Bonny moved at last, sighing restlessly, turning away from him slightly as she spoke.

"When I first pulled you back on to the path, you said you thought you'd be blamed," she said. "I didn't think

271

you'd be *blamed* – not exactly – but I thought you'd be saved a whole lot of questioning, and all for nothing, really. You'll laugh, but you always seemed so... unprotected. Not only from people like Nev, but from people like Janine, and from ideas as well – from visions, theories, all sorts of frenzies." She began tracing an outline on the edge of the table with her forefinger. "You were very imaginative..." She gave him a fleeting look, and went back to her invisible writing. "You were *sensitive*," she said defiantly. "But I shouldn't have told you to say you were up there on the path with me. I suppose I was still trying to be the Pythoness, giving advice."

Sophie had successfully opened her biscuits.

"Look," she cried, waving the package at them. "Some of those nice whatsitsnames." She lost interest in the other parcel and set to work busily to get at the biscuits. In the end Bonny helped her.

"I thank you very much," Sophie said formally.

"They kept me overnight in the hospital," Jonny said, moving to a more ordinary topic, "and some sort of shrink came and talked to me and to my parents. I ended up going back twice and talking to him with them there, going over all this stuff, and it lost its feeling of being a terrible secret."

"Did your mother tell you to smile?" Bonny asked.

"Look, they did their best," Jonny said severely. "It's tough on them, because after all they don't want me to prove any great theory about life, just to get a job and have a nice time and be no trouble. It's not much to ask."

"It's too much," said Bonny. "They don't want you to use your power."

"What power?" Jonny asked sarcastically. "The power to disturb the peace?"

"It has to be disturbed," Bonny said, "or there'd be nothing but boring old tranquillity. You just haven't found the right way to disturb it yet."

Sophie offered him a biscuit, and he took it, idly dipping it into his tea.

"Nana wouldn't have liked to see you do that," she told him sternly.

"Look, Jonny," Bonny said, leaning forward. "It's something I know about... I really do." She spoke rather sadly. "I'd like *your* power. I can recognise it when I see it in other people, when I see you, for example, thrashing around with it. But I don't have it myself. It's something to do with vitality or passion."

"They're very nice," Sophie said, taking another biscuit. "But you mustn't eat too many because of the refined sugar."

"You're allowed to, on your birthday," Jonny said, improvising. "You're allowed a treat." He thought of the curved flight of the Pythoness's ring, and remembered the moment when, a week or two later, he had found it once more lying lightly in the meadow grasses, as if it had just settled a moment earlier.

"You threw it away," he said, miming her action.

"It wasn't mine," Bonny said, understanding what he was talking about. "Not really. The only time it ever worked it foretold disaster. I wasn't really the Pythoness I was pretending to be. Did it help? Talking about it all, I mean?"

"I think it finished off something that was going to happen anyway," Jonny said. "I've thought a lot about it, on and off. I think things really began to change when I woke up on the traffic island, then met Sophie and came here. I think living in Sophie's house started it all off, but maybe I was ready to change, anyway. I can still remember Janine falling, but I don't remember it all the time the way I used to. It's got smaller."

"Smaller?"

"Different. It used to seem like a vision."

He didn't bother to say that he felt smaller too. In the beginning of this story, swollen with apparitions, he had stalked through the city and it had given in to him – had offered Bonny and Nev, to match up with the ghosts of memory. Exorcising these ghosts, he was set free of them at last. Yet he had lost something too, for part of their substance had come out of him in the first place. Besides, being haunted had had a seductive glamour about it. Jonny had seen there was a chance to escape from the desolate patches of life by becoming a demon, impervious to pain, but in the end he had dwindled back to being something more ordinary, and was glad to be restored.

Getting to his feet he began to walk around the room looking at the various changes that good housekeeping had brought about.

"Has it been difficult – looking after my friend, here?" he asked. He was talking to Bonny, but Sophie answered.

"Oh, no," she said. "He's a nice young chap, and besides, I think it's a poor lookout if we can't do something to help one another."

"Max Dainton says that twenty-four hour care is really needed," Bonny said, "and he's right. She sometimes wanders at night – well, you know all about that. But there are no places in any home for her. She'll have to wait her turn and, besides, in some ways it's really nice for her to be here as long as she possibly can. Max says he'll check on her regularly. I don't do much, but I can check up, too. At least I'm not just watching from the side."

"I thought I might move back," said Jonny casually, not daring to look at Bonny too directly. "I could make myself useful. Not all the time. I've got a bit of work at present. I've been working on a construction site in town for the last two weeks. Dad managed to find someone who'd take me on. I'm helping to finish off the excavation. I mean, the machines have moved out and we're just finishing off, before they pour the concrete. I push barrowloads of clay from one place to another, make tea, run errands, help shift scaffolding, all that sort of thing. It's walking distance from here."

Sophie was quietly sneaking yet another biscuit for herself.

"You thought you might come back and live here?" Bonny exclaimed. She laughed. "Oh, no! I don't believe it."

"Why not? I've got to leave home some time," Jonny said. "You wouldn't mind putting me up for a bit, would you, Sophie? I'd be no trouble."

"You are welcome at any time," Sophie said. "There's nothing like one of your own."

"You see – I'm one of her own," Jonny exclaimed. "I can make her breakfast and dinner at night. I mean, I'd be out during the day, but she'd be no worse off than she is now. A bit better off, actually." At last he looked up and met Bonny's eyes, fixed on him with an expression so ironical that he could not meet it for long, and glanced away, trying to look casual.

"Who do you think you're fooling?" Bonny asked. "Jonny, it's a mad idea. You're not the sort of person who ought to be tied down to looking after Sophie. You'll want to go out in the evening and rage around. You need a place where you can invite friends in, where you can play loud music or give parties."

"I'll go out when I want to," Jonny said. "Like I said, she won't be any worse off if I do, and some of the time she'll be better off. I'm not planning to turn into a nurse. Just be around. It'll be a lot better than nothing."

He had found it hard to explain just why he was so

Bonny turned in the doorway.

"They think I'm doing a very Maori thing, helping to
ok after an old woman – a *kuia*," she said. "Respect for
ders, and attention to old people is a Maori thing. They
ink I'm finding my origins at last. But I tell them it
ght be the Chinese bit."

"My mum takes good care of my granny," Jonny said.
nd you, my granny is as sharp as a tack. Sharper."

onny left. Jonny stood behind the closed door
ning to her footsteps go a few paces down Marribel
. He heard her door open and close. "Bonny
dicta," he muttered, "I reckon your engineer doesn't
a chance." But he knew it was something he could
ord to speculate on.

nding at the foot of the stair, listening to the silence
ie's house and the roar of the one-way street, Jonny
powerful. He felt as if he had died, and had then
rn again with his own death dissolved into his
rculating through his heart at seventy beats to the
contained and under strict control for a while.

mbed the stairs again thinking that, although he
sociable enough, he was really as Bonny had
herself, off to one side. He felt like a solitary
a world which sometimes came at you with a
f teeth wanting to tear your throat out, but which
sighed and lamented, "Oh dear, oh dear, oh
ble to cope with its own difficulties. On the face

interested in Sophie, or the imaginary world of Uncle
Brian and Errol and Alva whose identity he had shared. In
return for an independent place to stay he could keep an
eye on Sophie, entertain and feed her a little. He would
also have Bonny for a neighbour. Looking across the table
at Bonny in her black trousers, floppy jersey, her hair tied
back, he realised that he did not know her at all. Since it
seemed that she was his opposite in many ways, he would
have to find out about her in real life, find out what the
cave of books meant to her. He would have to learn to
understand her family, as mixed, it seemed, as his own.

"Jonny, I don't want to sound conceited," she said, "but
you're not thinking of coming back here because of me, are
you?"

"Hey, who's fishing for compliments this time?" Jonny
said cheerfully. "Mind you – if you wouldn't mind
babysitting from time to time…"

Bonny continued to stare at him very narrowly indeed,
but she did not look unfriendly. Her original, amused look
had come back, and though it was not the look that he
wanted from her, he was happy to see it on this occasion
because it was a beginning.

"Because you're not quite my style, and besides, I've got
a boyfriend," Bonny said. "You know that."

"Good on you," Jonny replied. "I suppose he's one of
those intellectuals."

"He's an engineer," said Bonny.

Jonny whistled scornfully. "An engineer!" he cried. "No wonder you feel too tranquil. When you come home tired after a day at the library, you don't want someone who can talk about stresses in bridges and things like that. You want someone lighthearted... someone who can go shuffling to Buffalo." As he spoke, he danced the step he had named. Bonny laughed and shook her head, and the light moved warmly over her, deepening the honeysuckle bloom of her forehead and high cheekbones.

"It's not going to last around here," she said. "Well, only another year or so. Even if nothing else happens we'll all run out along with the lease, and they'll bulldoze Tap House to dust. And goodness knows what else might happen."

"A year!" Jonny exclaimed. "A year! If it lasts a year that'll be terrific. I mean I've been thinking about a month ahead – well, say six weeks, recently. And before that I'd wake up in the morning hardly able to see to the end of the day. It's not as if I've got a great career mapped out, or anywhere much to go."

"You could take up dancing again," Bonny suggested, smiling. "That should go over well on the construction site."

"You can laugh," Jonny replied, "but I have been taking a few lessons again... not for any reason except – well, once you know something it's a pity to let it all go. And when I really get into it, I *know* I'm holding the world together."

He clapped his hands together, not looking at her

directly, watching Sophie trying to get anoth of the packet without being noticed.

"You know, Jonny – I have to adn remarkable in your way," Bonny said.

"Yes, you are," Sophie agreed surprisin another biscuit.

"Are you planning on staying her asked, looking at his carrier bag.

"I brought a few things," said Jonı toothbrush here."

"Then I'll go," Bonny said, "beca and someone's coming round later

"I wasn't going to ask," said J That's *Scorched Earth Policy* nigh

"What?" Bonny asked disbeli

"*Scorched Earth Policy*. It' Remember I stand in for thei usually go to listen to the rel far from here. I might ever wants to come. It could be experiences for you, Soph!"

As he saw Bonny dow Sophie settled down wit music often described a

"I suppose your pa extra responsibilities," two sets of teeth at or

of it, it wasn't likely that he would be able to live happily with Sophie for long, yet she linked up with knowledge he already had: that in their essence people were born and lived and died alone, and though this should have been a sombre thought, Jonny was in that mood when naming and mastering any piece of truth is its own consolation. He bounced into the sitting room, startling Sophie, who leaped to her feet spilling biscuits on to the floor.

"How did you get in?" she cried.

"You *let* me in," Jonny told her, picking up the biscuits. "You invited me in. Now I'm here to stay for a while. It shows how careful you've got to be."

"That's nice," said Sophie in a puzzled voice. "Do I know you?"

"I'm one of your own," Jonny explained. "I might go out in a moment, and you can come with me if you like."

Sophie's face brightened.

"That would be nice," she said, "and if we're going past the post office we could just pop in and get some money out because I always like to have something in the house, just in case..."

"It's shut," Jonny said, putting the biscuits on a plate. One or two of them looked a little bit dusty. "I thought we might catch a bus and go and listen to a band."

"Oh, yes," Sophie cried enthusiastically. "Errol loved bands. He loved to hear the Railway Workshop Band play *Land of Hope and Glory.*"

"Things have moved on since then," Jonny said. "You're in for a surprise. Go and pop on your coat, Sophie, and we'll see what we shall see."

Waiting for her, he idly rinsed the tea cups. Running away to see what we shall see, he thought. You can't see more than that.

There was a shuffle at his elbow. Sophie stood there wearing her hat and carrying her handbag, but instead of a coat she had pushed herself into a crocheted bed-jacket. One arm was coming out of an armhole, but the other had been pushed out at the neck, so that she was almost choked by some of it, while the rest of it hung down in a bright, limp pouch under her arm.

"We might have to make a few adjustments," Jonny said after a moment. "You need your coat." He began to help her out of the bed-jacket again.

Sophie was staring at him, looking pleased, but puzzled, too.

"Are you the one?" she suddenly asked incredulously. Jonny stopped and thought of the difference between being asked this question the first time, and being asked it now.

"Sophie," he said at last, "I think I *am* the one. I truly think I am."

And at that moment, although he could not say why, he knew, beyond all doubt, that he was one of the world's lucky ones.